TUNNEL

OF

GOLD

Lost Treasure of Petersburg

James B. Arnold

This publication is designed to provide accurate and authoritative information with regard to the subject matter covered.

Readers of this book should not act or refrain from acting on the basis of any information included herein without seeking appropriate legal or other relevant advice related to the particular facts and circumstances at issue from an attorney or other advisor duly and properly licensed in the recipient's state of residence.

TABLE OF CONTENTS

Table of Contents 3

A Note from the Author 7

Introduction 8

Cast of Characters 9

Prelude 11

Winter 1865 - Petersburg, Virginia..............11

Chapter 1 21

1974 - Petersburg, Va. 21

Chapter 2 23

Petersburg, VA 23

Chapter 3 25

Petersburg, Va. – 1864 25

Chapter 4 29

July 18, 1974 Petersburg, Va. 29

Chapter 5 33

The Choice..33

Chapter 6 37

Petersburg, Va. 1864..37

Chapter 7 40

1816 - Lexington, Kentucky 40

Chapter 8 47

Joe 47

Chapter 9 52

Joe's Vision 52

Chapter 10 56

Back to Work 56

Chapter 11 58

March 1863 - The Protectors 58

Chapter 12 62

Protector Training 62

Chapter 13 65

The Mission 65

Chapter 14 67

August 1863 – Time to Go 67

Chapter 15 71

Rosie B...71

Chapter 16 79

The Arrival 79

Chapter 17 82

April 14, 1865 The Explosion 82

Chapter 18 85

The Dig: End of an Era 85

Chapter 19 87

1976 Petersburg, VA 87

1980 Four Years Later...................................90

Chapter 21 93

August 16, 1980 Rainbows End 93

Epilogue 102

1985 103

Summer 103

Petersburg, Virginia 103

SAMPLE James B. Arnold's Next Book: ..106

Finding The Lost Dutchman's Gold 106

BOOK #2 of the 106

Tunnel of Gold Series 106

About the Author 116

Connect with James B. Arnold, Jr............117

A NOTE FROM THE AUTHOR

I was born in Petersburg, Virginia in 1954 and lived there for 26 years. During my teenage years, I worked for a painting and remodeling company. Along with other employees, I scraped, sandblasted, sanded and burned off 100 years of old paint on the wood surfaces of an old run-down house. The plan was to revitalize the building into the beautiful mansion the City of Petersburg could be proud to own and display as a museum for citizens and tourists to visit. The house was steeped in history and had yet to divulge many of its secrets. It was now called "Centre Hill Museum". During some remodeling work of the basement, life became very interesting. While most of the story is a work of fiction, there is much that is true and fact. You decide.

INTRODUCTION

Gold.... finding the tiniest speck puts a smile on the face of the bearer. Gold quickly creates wealth out of poverty and changes lives. Thousands upon thousands of men have died throughout time while searching for the yellow riches only to have it snatched out of their grasp; their dreams, and in many cases, their lives. Often being shattered by greedier men. Undaunted, others always arrived to take their place. There was always a long line of searchers, prospectors, and hunters looking to find that big deposit that would change the course of their lives and maybe history.

The story here is different only because this gold is intended to strengthen a nation. Here was more gold than a hundred men could dig in a lifetime. Wooden boxes, large chests, and steamer trunks full of gold bricks, coins, and freshly poured gold waiting to become new money or a piece of fine jewelry. Maybe some of it was made into pocket watches that would be destined to become a family heirloom or a pair of wedding bands that displayed the endless love of the wearers. But this gold was some of the purest gold mined in the United/Confederate States to date. A large amount of this yellow treasure came out of San Francisco from the California Gold Rush in 1848. But almost as much would be coming from just about every working mine in the country, crated in unmarked chests bearing only the initials UCSA. This gold was being collected by certain individuals for a singular expressed purpose. The gold in this convoy was more valuable than the total treasury of many small countries. It would bypass the normal wagon routes and the normal shipping routes. This gold had a different, special purpose unlike any before it. The cargo in these wagons contained the wealth of a nation, and in some cases, several nations. A sack full of this gold could make any of the men guarding it wealthy for the rest of their lives. However, this gold shipment was more protected than any cargo anywhere on earth and very few people even knew the contents of these crates, and even fewer knew the purpose for which it was being collected. In 1865, two unlikely men conspired to amass the largest gold collection ever attempted in recorded history. A failure could result in the collapse of a nation, maybe two.

CAST OF CHARACTERS

John Hawkins – Foreman in charge of Centre Hill renovations

Joe Bryant – Man of Skills, Great Grandson to Colonel DeKay

Colonel Arthur B. DeKay – Creator of Protectors, Great Grandfather to Joe

Henry Taylor – CSA Retired, Skilled Tracker and Mule Team Driver

David Nash – CSA Private

Robert Yates – CSA Private

Rosie Butler – Saloon owner, Friend to the Protectors

Ernie Cato – Crane Operator

Clarence Stevens – Crane Operator

Tate Larson - Sodbuster

Sam Larson – Sodbuster, brother of Tate

Abraham Lincoln – President of the Union States

Jefferson Davis – President of the Confederate States

General Robert E. Lee – Commander of the Army of the Confederate States

General Ulysses S. Grant – Commander of the Army of the Union States

Captain Bill Povandra – Union Officer Retired, friend of Colonel DeKay

Captain George Rogers – Union Officer Retired, friend of Captain Povandra

Petersburg Bureau of Police Officers – Security

Holt Armored Truck Division - Guards

Instructors

Gilly "Bear" Hanson -- Strength/Fighting

James "Horse" Carr -- Horse Tamer/Rider

Walt "Snake" Jones--Noiseless/Knife Expert

Ariel "One Shot" Myers--Shooting/Pick Pocket

Protectors

All Protectors shoot with Master Precision

Lindsey Berry – Female Protector – Very Skilled Kung Fu Master/Killer

Brana Arnold – Female Protector – Genius/Expert Bow

Tasha Evans – Female Protector – Seduction/Pressure Point Killer

Blake Smith - Male Protector – Very Skilled Tracker/fighter/Killer

Thomas Cole – Male Protector – Gadget Man/Hearing

Axle Andrews – Male Protector – Running/Jumping

William Armstrong – Male Protector – Acrobatics/Knives

Parker Reynolds – Male Protector – Muscle/Sight

PRELUDE

WINTER 1865 - PETERSBURG, VIRGINIA

Near the end of the Civil War

This night was a record bone chilling cold. The kind of cold where your breath freezes in your nose and on your eyelids. Wearing a cloth across your mouth did little to keep your face warm because it froze solid within seconds from your breath's exhalations. All the trees are leafless and frozen. Ice dangles from the tiny barren limbs. And dark. Real dark. The kind of charcoal dark that only a night with no moon and solid cloud cover can bring in the dead of winter. The air temperature was holding steady about 22 degrees with four inches of frozen snow on the ground. You could hear the "crunch" from the horse's hooves on the snow and their heavily labored breathing long before you could physically see them approach. Men and horses alike were nearing the end of a long treacherous journey. A journey filled with excitement, fear, dread and of course death. This was a journey like no other during the civil war and maybe even history. The horses were sweating profusely and spouting hot breath steam similar to an engine on a locomotive as if they had just finished running the last 10 miles instead of simply pulling the heavily laden wagons. Four horses pulled each wagon and had long tentacles of ice dripping down from their manes, tails, and belly. Each horse wore a thick wool blanket to help fight the extreme cold. The blankets were also covered in ice. It took all the strength they possessed, struggling to climb the hill toward the tunnel entrance.

Most of the men and women that began this journey made it to the end. A few good souls lost their lives in this endeavor, but that was to be expected.

The survivors are exhausted but happy to finally be here, close to the end of the line. For most of those involved, this was home, and the end of a journey that seemed to last a lifetime. One hell of an assignment to be sure.

As the handpicked team of civilians and cavalrymen brought the horse drawn heavy wagons up to the entrance of the tunnel, they were met by twenty of the most ruthless confederate soldiers that Henry Taylor had ever seen in one place. Their uniforms (if one dared call them that) were frayed, torn, mismatched and in general, the worst uniforms he ever saw. Shoes and boots were never meant to be worn this long. Some had no shoes at all, just feet wrapped in whatever cloth that could be scrounged or shoes that had been taken off a dead body, the ends cut off to accommodate a larger foot. Most had holes and tears and were patched with whatever they could find that would make them last a little longer. Each man hoped the war would be over real soon. Few wore coats. Most had old blankets wrapped around their shoulders attempting to save every scrap of body heat they could. Staying warm was next to impossible; they were already tired and hungry. They only dreamed of home-cooked warm meals. A table set with food-a-plenty was a long-forgotten vision. As with any war, each of them carried the same thought that they could not shake. Will today be my last day alive? and When will death come? These men and women had seen plenty of death and hoped they would not have to see anymore.

Henry Taylor had driven his wagon across the entire country and back. He swore he had changed so many wheels, axles, and horses that he lost count.

Henry had fought for the confederacy before he had been recruited for this mission. Henry was 35 years old, looked 45. He had a full beard that was mostly gray and white, premature for his age. Henry had a three-inch scar just below his right ear from a knife fight that he would boast about. He would regale those who would listen with his story about getting it during a fight with an Apache warrior.

The truth was, he did get it from an Apache, but she was 21 years old and very jealous. But that was another story. Henry had been promoted to the rank of Sergeant just before the beginning of this adventure.

He had grown up near Charleston, South Carolina in a small home and a few acres of land that his family farmed. They grew lots of vegetables and watermelon. Every year they would load the wagons and sell the fruit of their crops to the city folk. Henry's father would set the price for each combination of vegetables and make sure Henry and his sister knew exactly what to do. When Henry was about 15 years old his father was riding their horse and the saddle strap broke and his father fell and hit his head on a rock, killing him instantly. Henry learned farming well from his father and stayed on the farm until war broke out, and then he enlisted. His family never owned slaves but did have help from a black family that lived down the road. The fathers name was Joseph and he made his living farming with Henry's family. Joseph also joined the civil war and fought for the Confederacy. Henry's mom Anne and Joseph's wife Patrice worked the farm and sold the crops as best they could in the men's absence.

Considerably older than most soldiers, Henry was one of the most trusted men in the "inner circle" and had been hand-selected for this mission because of that trust. Henry was one of two men that possessed the most important documents in the entire civil war. Once his wagons were unloaded and the shipment was safe, he was to attach and seal his document to one of the crates. Henry along with his wife Georgia and their three children lived in a small cabin on a hill overlooking Wilcox Lake (Branch). Henry was originally from an area of Petersburg that is now known as "Walnut Hill". He was finally close to home. Reaching his destination, he was staring at what was supposed to be the most trustworthy men in the company. Henry wasn't very pleased with the looks of these men, but hey, he knew very well that looks weren't everything. He simply had to believe in those above his pay grade to know what they were doing. When they pulled up to the off-load site, they could see about 25 men milling around. Most appeared to be freezing cold and muttering under their breath.

The men started off-loading the wagons and noted how heavy the wooden crates were. A skinny fellow came walking up to assist in the unloading and Henry asked his name. Robert Yates the man said. Yates was scrawny but of average height. He had not seen a barber for a haircut or shave in weeks. Yates was of a questionable background but had never done anything outright dishonest, or so anyone knew. He was born and raised just across the Appomattox River outside the City limits of Petersburg in a small village called Ettrick Banks. It is now called Ettrick. The village was comprised of mostly Scottish descendants in 1765 and grew very slowly over the years. Robert's family was very poor during his childhood. His father worked in the cotton mill as a maintenance worker. He also kept most of the machinery greased and running. He could walk to the cotton mill as it was about three blocks from his home. Robert had almost no other children to play with because of the small village. As a child, he would go down to the Appomattox River and catch frogs, tadpoles, and worms. As he got older, he learned to fish and would spend his time fishing. Usually when he was supposed to be in class. However, his mother was always grateful for the fish as it gave them food for the table. Robert never spent a lot of time with his father. His father worked long hours at the mill and was always tired when he was home. Robert joined the Confederate Army when he was 17 years of age.

Yates reached over the back of the wagon and grabbed a rope handle to pull the box and stopped. He then exclaimed, "Crates of this size should not be this heavy". What in tar nation is in these boxes, rocks? Cannon balls? Each 2' x 2' box took two men to carry. The crates were made of wood reinforced at each corner with cast iron straps and had thick iron handles on each end. When Yates grabbed the first box to slide it off the back of the wagon it almost threw him over his own shoulder.

"Good Grief!" he yelled, "David, get over here and grab the other end."

Yates' buddy, David Nash said, "What a weakling! Let me in there!"

David grabbed the box and almost pulled his arm out of its socket."Holy Smokes," he stated, "Are all these crates this heavy"?

He stopped and counted ten wagons with 15 crates on each; he thought that's got to be 60 or 70 crates in all. His math wasn't very good. After all, he only went to the second grade.

David said, "That's closer to 120 crates, your math ain't so good."

Now, David Nash had been reared by his Uncle Jeremiah West. Jeremiah had been in the steel business in Pennsylvania and retired to Petersburg in 1842. His brother Joseph and Cecilia (David's parents) had been killed by a runaway wagon later that same year. David had recently been born when his parents were killed so his uncle was just like his father to him. David had nice things growing up including lots of friends. He always had an adventurous spirit. He loved to climb trees and swing out over the river and drop in the water, pretending he was a pirate landing on a ship. As soon as the war broke out, he clambered to get to town and sign up to join the war effort. David thought it very glamorous. His uncle was proud of him for serving his country. David liked being in the tunnel. He found it exciting and would daydream about capturing a bunch of Union troops and keeping them here. They had been using the tunnel from under the house as a makeshift place meet and to get out of the cold

The tunnel was dug into the side of a hill near the Appomattox River at the North end and ended underneath the Centre Hill House in the basement at the Southern end. It had been dug as an escape exit out of a basement down toward the Appomattox River. It was about 200-feet long, 10-feet wide and higher than seven feet, so most men could stand and run if needed. Lanterns spraying their light throughout, dangled on both sides of the tunnel spaced about 10 feet apart. The closer you got to the house, the more lanterns were hung, and the more light there was. The walls of the tunnel were of reinforced brick and heavy timber for stability; a damp musty smell wafted throughout.

Many large homes throughout Virginia had secret tunnels where owners could hide from attackers including Indians, renegades and Yankees. Some were attached to the house while others were a short distance away from the home. In this tunnel, two rooms had been carved out of the dirt walls close to the house foundation.

One was about the size of a small bedroom, built to house supplies, and the other, about half that size across the hall, was designed to be hidden. When the door was closed, it blended with the walls becoming hidden unless one got very close, searching for the almost imperceptible crack. At one time the tunnel could be accessed from a closet upstairs in the kitchen. The closet was disguised as a broom closet with a very slender door that any large man would be unable to enter. Once inside, a hatch in the floor could be raised up. A wooden ladder ran down to the floor of the tunnel for quick escapes. A clever sign hung on the door that read: Mops, Buckets and Brooms. This discouraged anyone from opening the door and finding the tunnel. But if they did open the door all they would see was mops and such.

All the men were working hard and blowing puffs of white breath to prove it. It took 20 men several trips each to unload the crates and get them stacked inside the dirt room. Most were dripping sweat even though it was very cold. The men were directed to place the crates in the larger room. When they were close to being finished, David and Robert were placing the last crate on top of the pile. David dropped his end and Robert yelled, "Look out! Let it go!"

The crate tumbled about three feet and landed on its corner, breaking open, just a little. The two men stared down at what fell out. Lying on the dirt floor, were several shiny coins. There must have been fifteen to twenty of them. Solid gold Twenty Dollar Double Eagle, coins. Alone now, David and Robert looked to see where the other soldiers and officers were. To their excitement, everyone had already walked out to get some fresh air.

"You see what I see?" Robert asked.

Thinking they couldn't be real David reached down and grabbed a hand full. He raised his hand, bringing them up to his eyes to get a better look. As he began putting them back into the crate, Robert, who was afraid to even speak whispered, "Are they real?"

"Well, they seem awfully real to me. I ain't never touched one this new before, but it bites the same as real."

David bit down on the coin. It was soft.

"They sure look and feel real to me," he answered handing a few to Robert.

"I see what you mean, these are brand new!" Robert sputtered. "Well, don't just stand there, let's get them back in this box before anyone sees us. If'n we get caught with these coins in our hands they'll hang us for sure like we was thieves. Just then, the two heard a lot of commotion outside the tunnel near the entrance. Colonel Arthur B. DeKay rode up and the men snapped to attention!

"At ease, men!" he shouted.

"Sergeant Taylor, please inform your men that they will only be unloading five of the wagon's here."

He continued without taking a breath.

"The other five will be driven to the train depot and placed on a box car where I have a small band of men waiting there now!"

As the other two wagons started off, Robert looked at David and sighed with relief.

"I'm sure glad we don't have to unload all 10 wagons.

David said, "Come on. The sooner we get these unloaded, the sooner I can go and get some sleep."

Robert didn't look up, "I got to stay here all day. You go on and get some sleep." Shortly after, David left to lie down. Robert went back to his normal duties which included guarding the tunnel.

Robert enjoyed walking into the basement on hot days because it was very cool down there. If he opened the closet door, a pleasant breeze would flow through the tunnel and he could sleep in the comfortably cooler air. Of course, it was freezing everywhere in the tunnel this time of year.

On this particular night, since everyone else was busy, he went to his favorite napping spot to catch a few winks and try to get warm.

As it turned out he had trouble going to sleep. All he could think about was the gold. After a while, deciding he had better things to do than sleep, he came up with an idea.

He rummaged around in the kitchen trash and found what he was looking for, a few empty flour sacks. Slipping into the room full of the crates, he found the broken crate and decided it would not hurt anything if he took a few gold coins for himself. He rationalized that he would not be greedy, and furthermore, surely, a few coins would not be missed. When he finished his deed, ten small sacks of coins, each about the size of his fist, were in neat rows at his feet. Just then, a voice cried out, "What are you doing?" Robert froze! He turned around and David laughed out loud, "Hee Haw! You look like you just swallowed the canary!"

"Damn! You scared me, Robert said, "I thought you was the Colonel.

Well, David, what ARE you in here doing?"

"I couldn't sleep. I was thinking I might come and see if you needed some help." Robert stared at David.

"Oh, bullshit," Robert said, "You was thinking about this gold, you were. I know you. I thought you might come and git a piece or two for yourself."

David grew quiet for a moment.

"I guess...well.... I was thinking I never seen so much gold and just got to wondering how much it is worth."

The small sacks of coins were too heavy to carry all at once, so he made three trips. Robert knew the tunnel and basement better than anyone. He found a special place to hide them where only he could find them. David loaded two sacks with gold coins and was walking through the tunnel toward the river when the ground began to shake.

Suddenly, he heard what sounded like a tremendous explosion. The roaring in his ears would not stop.

The ground started shaking and vibrating and seemed to go on forever. Brick, dirt and dust poured down from all over. He could not see anything for the dust. The noise was deafening. Timbers and bricks were falling on top of men, crushing them instantly, shattering skulls and earsplitting screams of agony filled the air.

The wood supports at the lower end of the tunnel blew apart and the entire hillside collapsed taking about more than 60 feet of tunnel, and men with it. David was thrown through the doorway of a side room, deafened by the dirt and rock tumbling on top of him.

At least half the hillside was gone. Robert was thrown to the floor and had been completely covered in rock and dirt. He could not get his breath; his mouth and nose were full of dust and dirt. In those few seconds, that stretched out like hours, he saw his life pass before his eyes. His ears were ringing so loudly that he could not hear anything else. Disoriented, Robert was confused, trying to determine what was happening. They both had the same thought, EARTHQUAKE! But they never had serious earthquakes in this part of Virginia. With his mouth full of dirt, breathing was nearly impossible and his chest felt like he had a house sitting on top of him.

Robert would never know what happened, because just then, at that moment, he attempted to draw his final breath but only inhaled more dirt. He lost consciousness and died never knowing the truth of what happened, that this was no earthquake. He would simply become another victim of gold fever.

CHAPTER 1

1974 - PETERSBURG, VA.

House of Many Secrets

Having stood empty for many years, succumbing to great disrepair of rotting and buckling wood, broken windows, cracked and broken brick, and paint peeling, not to mention the abuse by local vandals, the once proud "Centre Hill House" was finally being restored to its original beauty. Rich in Virginia heritage for all to see, the plan was to turn the house into a Civil War museum for the City of Petersburg, Virginia.

No one living knew the secrets the old house heard during its lifetime. Certainly, none were more important than those heard during the many civil war meetings. The house was a silent listener to secrets of a nation's conspiracies. The walls overheard tales of wealth, slave trading, and life in modern 1800's America, and of everyday survival. Important men whose stories changed the course of history and the nation passed through the halls. One day, this house would divulge some of its secrets solving some 100 years' old mysteries, and again become an important link in understanding historical events, marking its rightful place in American history.

Before very long, the house would soon disclose a sight unseen for many years. In short sequence, scenes and secrets, held only by a very select few, long dead, individuals would shine one day soon for all to see. Named "Centre Hill Museum", it sits on top of the highest hilltop near downtown Petersburg. The mansion overlooks the lower half of a mostly refurbished older business district. The Appomattox River, which is a few short blocks away, flows below its stately perch. In those days, the front of such homes were built to face the water, which in this case, was the shipping route into Petersburg. Centre Hill was no exception. Hundreds of men died fighting the Civil War just around the bend from its watch. From the south looking north toward Richmond, the porch offered a sweeping expanse. There, soldiers could monitor General Grants Army for more than a mile, another unintended purpose for the home's porch during this time.

CHAPTER 2

PETERSBURG, VA

1837 Old Centre Hill House

      The Old Centre Hill House was built in 1823 by a Retired Revolutionary War Colonel, Robert Bolling IV. Bolling was born in 1759 in Petersburg, Virginia. His family was among the first settlers of Jamestown and was one of the earliest prominent families in the establishment of Petersburg. His Great Grandfather, Robert Bolling I, married Jane Rolfe, who was the Granddaughter of Pocahontas. The mansion's architectural style of building includes Greek Revival, Italianate, and Colonial Revival. The front and back of the home look very similar. The back of the home faces North toward Richmond which served as the Capital of the Confederacy during the Civil War. The view is magnificent. Centre Hill was a testament of wealth with its rich brick exterior, oversize windows, French doors, rooftop Widow's walk, and decorative dentil blocks. It was built to withstand Old Virginia's thunderstorms, ice storms, and the occasional hurricane.

      Each window was covered with sturdy seven-foot tall wooden shutters that, when closed, would encase the mansion in darkness, but protect it like a fortress from Indian attacks, thieves, heavy snowfall and other severe weather. Two full stories perched atop a basement with 12 foot ceilings, serving its owner proud. Its beauty attracted such glorious affairs as weddings, recitals, and elaborate dinner parties of the elite.

Even though centrally located, it was very well hidden among the green Virginia landscape sitting back at the end of a bluff with a narrow entryway accessing the property. When the trees were in full bloom, the house was practically invisible from the main roads and afforded great privacy to all those who visited. The front yard (or back yard, depending on which way you thought about it) was covered with tall pines and full, lush Dogwoods. In early summer, dogwoods displayed a beautiful mixture of pink and white blossoms which made the house difficult to see from any distance. Mr. Bolling also planted "Pecan" trees (pronounced Pee'can in the South) over the entire front acreage. Their fruit could be eaten raw or cooked in desserts, offering a hardy snack to many a soldier. Several beautiful oaks adorned the front edge of the lawn as well.

CHAPTER 3

PETERSBURG, VA. – 1864

Comfort, strength, and its secrecy, became three main reasons Presidents Jefferson Davis and Abraham Lincoln chose the home for a meeting that was sure to change the country. The two great men had shared a common friendship since childhood. They also shared a love for this beautiful country.

During the 1800's, Presidents rarely traveled with any type of bodyguard and the secret service had not yet been born. It would take the death of a great president to make that happen. Having located the tunnel from the river, the two great men decided this would provide them with cover and anonymity for safe passage and meeting. The house had been cleared and guards were posted just beyond 100 yards from the home; its shutters fully closed and lamps turned low. The two were led into the formal dining room. Thirteen-foot ceilings stretched up to meet its extraordinarily large chandelier in the center made of beautiful crystal glass with clear candle holders. The walls were painted a light green color on top with a darker green panel on the bottom separated by a multi layered chair rail. The floors were wide oak planks polished to a high gloss reflecting a roaring fire leaping from the fireplace against an outer wall. The two men sat down at a large handmade oaken table large enough to seat eight people comfortably. Colonel DeKay had left them water, tea, and

Kentucky whiskey on one side of the table and fresh smoked ham, biscuits and gravy, butterbeans, rice and pecan pie for dessert on the other side. Both men smiled. God love Colonel DeKay! Abe said, "Well, we might as well partake of these wonderful vittles."

Jeff agreed saying, "You serve, I'll pour the whiskey!"

"I think you are going to like what I have put together for this great country of ours," Abe told Jeff.

"It still needs your finishing touch, but I really think we have the best plan for the rebuild and reuniting."

With that, Jeff handed Abe his drink, and Abe exchanged it for a document that he laid on the table. Jeff raised his glass to Abe and said, "Here's hoping that we can reunite this country, and bring the North and South together to become as close as you and me."

"This document should go a long way to that end," said Jeff his glass still raised high, " HERE! HERE!"

And then Jeff took one, last, long swallow and set down the empty glass.

"Mercy! That was tasty!" he said.

Abe opted for a much smaller taste and set his glass down launching into an oration regarding the evils of drink and how much he could find a way to enjoy a glass of whiskey on a regular basis. Although, he added, the missus certainly would not approve.

After one more drink, the two men ate until they were satisfied, and then pushed away from the table. "Could I get you to join me in a fine smoke, Abe?"

Someone who loved fine things, Jeff stated with a smirk, "Cuban cigars are one of my many weaknesses."

Abe shook his head, "I never developed a desire for the cigar, even though I do appreciate the smell once in a while. But you go ahead. Get comfortable and let's discuss the plan."

As Jeff lit his cigar with a fireplace match, Abe looked at Jeff squarely, and asked him, "What would you think if I told you that there might be a way to stop this dadblamed war?"

We both know so many sons and fathers have died, so many have left the farms short-handed. Terrible. Crops lay rotting in the fields. With women and children unable to tend to them, cattle have starved, been stolen or run off.

"Agreed," Jeff said seriously.

"I have also been witness to so many homes that have come into great disrepair simply because there is no one tending to them.

Abe said, "That is correct! Fine sir! Such a sorry state we both have on our hands."

"To put it simply," Abe said, "Point One. There might be a way to rebuild homes for those that lost their home during this war. Point Two. If we could provide jobs to all men, whole or disabled, we could return some lost pride and give them a chance to earn a fair living for themselves and their families. Point Three. We need to build more railways and roadways to move workers as quickly as possible in all directions. Point Four is the most difficult part of the plan. In Point Four, we need to treat all men and women as equals in every aspect. It's the only way if we are to unite this country as one where we are all Americans and have the strongest most powerful country in the world!

Abe looked over at Jeff, "Now Jeff, I know what you are thinking. You think I have lost all or part of my mind. I assure you I have studied this thing over and over and cannot figure a better way than this.

Jeff stared at Abe for three long minutes without saying a word.

Abe shifted in his chair; he was starting to worry. Maybe he had gone too far pitching his idea to his old friend?

Finally, Jeff shook his head and pointed his finger at Abe, grinning, an odd sort of grin that was fast becoming a full-on smile, and said, "If we can sell this to our Congress' we will still need the most difficult part to come together.

Then at the same time, both men said, "Financing!"

Both knew the plan would take lots of money that neither the North or South were able to afford.

"I think I just may have an idea that could solve some of that problem," Jeff said, But, it would take a lot of convincing to make it work."

Abe said, "Well, let's hear it. Surely, together we can spew enough dazzling soliloquy that we could make them agree with the idea just to make us stop talking!"

Then Jeff explained his idea, "We both know lots of multimillionaires that have excess money. We know we can sell stocks and create government bonds once our nation is back together. We can also set and regulate the gold standard for a tidy profit to the country. But above all else, we must move forward as one country. Agreed!

CHAPTER 4

JULY 18, 1974 PETERSBURG, VA.

Renovation of Centre Hill Mansion/Museum

Hundreds of years' worth of thick layers of paint covered the old structure's window trim, cornice overhangs, porch columns, and ceilings. The job of scorching off the layers with specially-designed gas torches took teams of workmen painstaking weeks to finish. Once the paint was removed, a fresh, brand-new coat would make the exterior of the house appear brand new.

The crews took great care not to set the very aged and rotted wood on fire as most of it predated the Civil War and could ignite as if fueled by gasoline if great caution was not exercised.

Preserving the integrity of the original structure was priority. This July day in 1974 was particularly hot and humid with temperatures reaching toward 100 degrees. The weather coupled with a fully-enclosed sandblasting suit, complete with hood made for a challenging job. Additionally, the propane gas torches further complicated things, making working on the exterior of the mansion especially difficult. But today was the day several of the workers were looking forward to. Today, the men completed the exterior burning and would be starting work in the basement. The basement, where it would be 15-degrees cooler! They couldn't wait.

Lead Foreman, John Hawkins, ran a tight crew. He was built like a bulldozer, average height at about five feet, nine inches, weighing in at just about 245 pounds.

With hands like vice grips, he was as strong as two men. And, he had a heart of gold. He always considered how his instructions affected the other men and he never asked anyone to do any job that he wouldn't stand beside them and do himself. At the time, his only real weaknesses were his love of country music and his three children. Oh, how he loved to hear Conway Twitty and Loretta Lynn sing a duet! No matter how hot the temperature was, if they came on the radio, John was sure to be overheard, joining in, and maybe even doing a little two-step and twirl with a twist. His dancing was only outshined by his sporting a great big smile.

Unfortunately, John couldn't sing a note. But, he never let that silly tidbit get in his way from making a great effort. Many a person laughed at his zealousness for song. John would simply smile, and then keep right on singing along with Conway highlighted by his little side-step shuffle every now and again. John always worked hard so his children could have plenty to eat and clothes. He loved his children but especially his youngest daughter, Linda. She was always by his side watching and learning. John's demeanor was just another reason why he and his sidekick and best friend of several years, Joe Bryant, got along so well. Joe was seven years younger and was stronger than average for his age and size. And while he still had not reached the limit of his strength, he was plenty strong for his age.

The two friends had regular "strong man" contests during lunch breaks taking bets from the other workers on who would win. Joe usually let John win, but no one was the wiser. From the time he was a child, Joe could remember being very strong, but he was never a braggart, nor did he show off, choosing instead to hide his exceptional strength to avoid attention. More on this later…

John came from a large family of all boys. Five to be exact. John was the second oldest and kept all the others in line. John's younger brother Clarence was the fighter. He looked for reasons to fight. When things went sour in a club you would want Clarence with you.

John was an amazing person. He could perform just about any task he chose and do it very well. Especially painting, remodeling homes, welding and motorcycle repair. He never called on anyone to fix something that he knew, if he messed with it long enough, he could fix himself. If he did not know how, he would learn. Being built like a bulldozer, very few men would anger him. He could hold his own and then some in a fight. If a fight broke out, he would yell, "Katie bar the door"! It's on now! But above it all John believed in doing the right thing and treating people with respect.

With the rest of the crew working upstairs, John and Joe started sandblasting and scraping paint off the basement walls. The person sandblasting had to wear a heavy long sleeve top and heavy pants, and a full helmet with a glass face plate that draped over your shirt. Most helmets had some type of fan inside to help with the heat. It would still reach over 100 degrees inside the suit. It could only be worn for short periods of time if you were working in the sun.

The thick, brick walls matched the exterior walls only they were caked with 30-plus layers of thick paint. The basement air was much cooler during the Summer months and the men took pleasure in getting as much relief from the heat as they could.

There was a tiny door that led into the basement at the left front corner of the house. This was the only entrance to the basement as there were no doors to it from inside the house. Brick "Arches" comprised the basement foundation for greater support using less building material. The arches style of construction also allowed for use of most of the basement area without walls. John and Joe went into the basement and assessed where to begin. The two men then brought all the hoses and equipment into the basement, getting it ready for their work. Joe did a double-take and noticed that something did not seem right about the size of the basement. He shook it off and quickly went back to work.

Among the two, John was much more experienced with this type of work, and he knew that they needed to take great care in sandblasting the 150-year-old brick to keep it from crumbling. This brick had been painted over so many times that its layers could be measured in inches rather than coats and it wasn't going to come off easily.

Joe got suited up while John loaded all the sand into the pump. After he cranked up the radio with some country music, John heard Joe grab the spray handle and yell to start the pump. Like a fire hose, this hose was difficult to hold once full pressure was applied. The sand shot out of the end at very high pressure literally "blasting" the paint off the walls and leaving very little else, if anything, in its wake. Too little pressure, and the paint wouldn't budge, too much pressure, and it would bore a hole right through the brick or wood. The sand blast operator had to be very careful not to hold the hose in one place for too long or a huge hole would be the result right through brick or wood. In the wrong hands, thee powerful jet of sand shooting out the end of the hose could create major problems.

While Joe was blasting, John would shovel the sand and paint particles into a wheelbarrow and then on to dump it into a sifter. The sand filtered through leaving the paint particles behind to be recycled. The paint debris could be hauled away. Both jobs were very labor intensive.

After about forty-five minutes of heavy blasting, the guys decided to take a break. While seated on buckets and eating a snack and drinking a Pepsi, Joe asked John if he knew anything about the house. John told him he thought the tourism department of the city had purchased the home with plans to open a Civil War Museum. John said he had played around the house as a child but never knew any more about it. Joe mused that the house had an unusual "feel" about it like it was hiding something. Shrugging off Joe's creepy feelings, John explained the eerry feeling was probably because the house was so old and, in such disrepair. Both men went back to work, John watching closely as Joe blasted the old brick walls, assuring the sandblaster did not penetrate the brick or remove too much mortar. "Pointing up" the mortar was next after blasting to make it solid and strong again. He was motivated to keep an eye on things, making sure they avoided creating any holes to fix.

During a break in the sandblasting Joe asked John about the solid brick arches and why they were used in the basement interior walls. These were not unusual in a basement of this type of home, however, typically, they would simply be support type arches and not filled-in interior walls. These odd arches appeared to close rooms off with filled-in brick. Waving his hand in the shape of the arch, John explained they supplied extra support for the main house foundation. After all, it was a large house and felt like it was built extra heavy duty. Joe resumed sandblasting. He couldn't stop thinking and wondering about the arches. Their mysterious secrets would stay hidden and guarded for more than 100 years. No one living knew the secrets.

That night, as Joe lay in bed, unable to sleep, his thoughts continually revisited the arches and basement walls. Joe was restless anyway. He knew what he wanted to do, what he must do.

CHAPTER 5

THE CHOICE

The Centre Hill Museum walls stood silent as the meetings and whispers of great men happened around them. They heard plans for great battles and discussions of the many men from both sides that had fallen. The floors absorbed the tears that fell as these leaders remembered the losses of both sides. Brother against brother fought protecting rights to a way of life that each held dear. If only these walls could talk. Great battle plans had been constructed here.

The house had far more secrets than anyone knew and although he didn't know it yet, Joe was about to learn some of them. The truths that had been hidden, that had changed many lives, were going to change many more, real soon. The morning arrived as an ordinary day. Joe suited up and prepared for another long day of filthy, hot, and sticky sandblasting. He began his blasting and moved slowly, inches at a time, across each layer of brick and mortar joints. He was careful to move the blasting gun ever so slowly while watching the white paint peel from the surface, exposing once bright red brick to the world again. This process was particularly slow to keep from damaging the beautiful brick underneath. Hour after hour of blasting. The entire time Joe continued to wonder about the arches and mysterious walls. At one-point Joe noticed the mortar crumbling out fast and stopped the blasting.

He then took out his putty knife and started to dig a little deeper.

"John!" Joe yelled through the hooded suit, "Fill the hopper with more sand!"

Suddenly, the sandblaster lurched and punched a small hole through the mortar seam, and Joe shut down the sandblasting gun.

He pulled off the hood and put his finger into the hole, expecting brick and felt nothing but air. There was a hollow area behind the hole. Curious, Joe put his nose right up to the hole, and could smell old musty air. "John!", Joe called, "Come over here and see this!"

John walked over and looked at the hole. "Smell the air," said Joe.

John took a whiff and said it smelled like old stale air inside.

"It's hollow", Joe said.

"We better patch it up and leave it alone before the museum curator comes in here and sees it,"

"The curator will be more concerned with the upstairs than down here," Joe told John.

"I think we should dig it out a little more and see if anything is inside," Joe said.

"No way, the boss would have our hide if he came in here and saw we had dug out a bunch of this old brick. Let's just patch it and keep going."

As John walked away and started scraping walls in the other room, Joe started picking out a little more of the loose edges of the mortar. In two minutes Joe had removed all the mortar around a whole brick and had slid the brick out easily. Immediately, Joe smelled the musty, stale smell that can only come with air trapped for long periods of time. It's the kind of stink that makes you turn your head and say "oouuwee"! Peering into the hole, Joe still couldn't see anything, but the air kept hitting him in the face with its smelly old yuck.

Drawing back, "I need a flashlight," and with that, Joe headed to the work truck glove box where he knew they kept one.

He retrieved the flashlight and went back down into the basement. John stood at the hole shaking his head. Then, he looked at Joe and said,

"Are you crazy?"

"I just want to look in the hole, Joe explained, "I'll put the brick right back and caulk it back into place."

Just then, the curator came into the basement to check on progress as John scraped the walls while Joe started up the sandblasting again. Joe knew the curator wouldn't be there long when he started blasting with dust and dirt flying everywhere. He quickly replaced the brick and kept on working.

Later that night in bed, Joe tossed and turned thinking about what might be inside that wall. Naturally, it could be only a space between the brick walls that contained nothing more than old air and dead bugs. If he knew that that is what existed there, he would be satisfied and could stop thinking about it. Still, an adventure was on its way, he could feel it. After he fell asleep, he dreamed he removed each brick with care, marking each one for replacement back in the hole. Before he knew it, he had removed forty bricks. In his dream, he aimed the flashlight into the hole, and looked inside.

"Holy Smokes!" he yelled. "John look at this!"

John rushed over, and together their eyes followed the beam of the flashlight. Gasping, they saw the light land on old wooden crates, rotted, falling apart, and spilling the contents on the dirt floor.

"Oh My Gosh," Joe exclaimed!

In that moment, the single beam of light reflected a brilliance that could mean only one thing: gold. Everywhere the light shone, thousands of gold coins lay about the basement floor. At least two of the crates appeared to contain bars instead of coin and far as the light would project, all they could see was the brilliance of gold.

This was not a room. instead it appeared to be a tunnel of some sort that continued beyond the distance of the light. As he spoke, Joe could hear his voice bouncing off the walls, slightly echoing.

He was about to explode with excitement. His curiosity pushed him and he began to crawl through the opening when Johns huge hand grabbed him by the collar and stopped him.

John said, "What are you doing?! You can't go in there. There could be snakes, or something, and we'll get caught and lose our jobs."

"I'm going in," Joe answered defiantly, "Just let me know if you hear anything. About halfway through the opening, Joe's right foot caught on the edge of the brick, tripping him. He landed on the dirt floor that had not seen moisture in a hundred years. A plume of dust rose and encased Joe in its thin, black, velvety residue.

John looked down at his coworker on the ground, "Are you alright?"

With a loud sneeze, Joe laughed and said he was fine.

"I'm just a little dirtier than normal." and with that, he jumped up and banged his head on a ceiling timber and saw lots of stars. Now he really was out cold.

CHAPTER 6

PETERSBURG, VA. 1864

The Virginia weather was beautiful this time of year; the dogwoods were in full bloom. Petersburg was noted for its vibrant pink and white colors throughout the city. Unfortunately, most of the trees had been damaged in some way, either because of cannon and rifle fire, or even the mighty ax. Just about every tree that could be used for fuel for warmth or cooking had been destroyed. Centre Hill did manage to save several dogwoods on the front lawn, mostly unscathed because the house and grounds had become a common meeting place for confederate staff.

Usually, the presidents of the time traveled with a secretary or aid that would take notes of everything the president said or did, and would courier when an errand needed to be run. On this particular day, both Presidents agreed, instead, to meet alone, and did not want any written record to follow them. The aids were left in a quandary sitting on the front porch drinking warm sweet tea. Sweet tea was a southern tradition. Tea leaves brewed for about thirty minutes and filtered, and finally water and sugar are added to taste.

The immediate area had been swept by the Army so that no stragglers were wandering close by. President Lincoln never told his staff why he wanted this done, just to make it so. Also, nobody knew a disguised President Davis was close by, outfitted to look like a wealthy Virginia landowner and politician.

He had been waiting for the signal that it was clear to come out of hiding and meet with Lincoln.

Abe was the first to speak.

"How is my old friend this beautiful morning?"

Jefferson responded, "I am very well, were it not for the weight of the heavy burden we carry upon us, we could be going on a fine Virginia hunt this morning."

Abe said, "You know, yesterday, I was pondering about the day we met. I decided that every life and every path of that life must be destined before birth. Any of a million circumstances could have changed what happened to us that day, but we met, and are here today because of that chance meeting. We have changed many lives over the course of our short lifetime. Fate is very real.

Jefferson said, "I think I agree with you my old friend. Any small circumstance or event could have changed the course of our lives, it's true, but here we are now, and here we have this monumental cause before us that we could mess up due to our foolishness."

"This dadblamed war has cost us dearly. Entire families are now gone. Good people that lived simple lives, and farmers that not only spent their days toiling over their land, but cared about their families and friends alike. Good, honest people I tell you! Wiped out! And for what? Hardheaded men with such differences of opinion that they couldn't agree on whether to swim or float the river to cross.

"This thing needs to be over soon. We've buried too many good men and destroyed too many families. Recovery is going to take a long time and everyone is tired and wants to go home. If this slaughter continues there will not be enough left to rebuild."

Abe nodded, "This thing should end soon enough. And yes, many a good man and family has been wiped out. I pray their souls redeemed. No man deserves to die in vain as so many have. It weighs upon us to get this war over quickly and to have enough capital to rebuild our great nation.

Wistful, Abe continued, "Life was so simple when we were young.

"Why did we make it so complicated and unfriendly?" asked Jeff.

"Do you really remember when we met? It seems to me that life was very uncomplicated back then. Of course, that time seems many lifetimes ago now."

"Ah," Abe replied, "But I think it's all relative. I think it really was very difficult for our parents. But, what a wonderful time it was to be a young boy. In fact, I remember that day very well, I think I was ……………….and we were………… **drifting off to years before.**

"Everything is changing   today,   and   becoming   so complicated," Abe pondered, again…. drifting into **1816…**

CHAPTER 7

1816 - LEXINGTON, KENTUCKY

It was a beautiful sunny day. The sky was the kind of blue that only a clear summer day in July can muster. Lexington, Kentucky was not a large city by the standards of the day and time but it was growing fast. There was a community fair followed by a late-night dance on Saturday night in the community square barn. Families from all over Kentucky and the better part of Illinois came out for the 3rd annual three-day event. Around noon on Saturday, a Turkey shoot was held for all ages starting with a youth category of ages five to seven years old. In today's world, unheard of and even frowned upon, but in 1816 America, hunting was a necessary way of life that young boys learn to shoot for survival. In the contest, five boys shot at a time, each at one of five targets, twenty feet away, consisting of a twelve-inch square piece of paper** mounted on an old rough cut hickory post sticking out of the ground about 4 feet. The concessionaire supplied the black powder rifles.

At the sound of the whistle, the competitors fired, the winner was the one that had shot closest to the target center. A chance encounter took place that day that would unknowingly alter the course of many lives. Two young boys that had never met were standing back watching the event, wishing they could have a try.

One of the boys was tall, about six inches taller than the other, with a large masculine face. The other boy, though shorter, was a little heavier in frame and had a kind face.

Neither boy had the money for the nickel entry fee. The taller of the two, was eating a piece of roasted corn rescued from the ground having been dropped by another child. The other boy, eyeing the ear, said he wished he could get one because he was hungry. With about one third of the corn left, the taller boy looked at his ear of corn, looked at the shorter boy, and handed it to him.

"Thanks, friend," he said.

The shorter boy's mother was standing a few feet away watching the commotion. She, too, looked as though she had not had a decent meal in some time and her clothes were old, but clean. A proud woman, she stood very erect appearing as though she were waiting for a carriage to stop and assist her. She had a gentleness about her, and her nature was one of kindness, always helping those in need.

She stood watching the boys as if she knew what was about to happen and didn't dare interrupt for fear the slightest signal from her would break the spell. Little did she know how right she was. After the first volley was over, and upon checking each of the five targets, the judges realized only one child had even come close to hitting the target, a tiny tear on an outside edge. And likely, that tear was probably not even intended by the shooter!

The taller boy shouted that his Grandma could shoot better than that! Soon, the shorter boy chimed in with his laughter and agreeing that his dog could have hit a target the size of that one.

The man working the shoot (Mr. Snead) was embarrassed scolding the boys to step up to shoot and give it a go or be quiet. Both quickly argued they did not have the entry fee but could shoot better than any others.

"Stand back everyone!" Mr. Snead exclaimed. "I've got two world famous shooters stepping up to the plate.

They claim they can shoot the target off the post!" Several of the last shooters yelled, "I would like to see them try!"

Mr. Snead said, "Boys, I'll tell ya what I'll do. I'll waive the entry fee and let ya have a go. If ya'll miss ya'll will work for me for two hours after I close the show."

Unable to believe their luck, the two boys looked at each other and jumped with excitement.

"Hey mister," they yelled! "You got a deal."

Each boy grabbed the pre-loaded firearms and carefully took aim. The sun was shining brightly, and the taller boy sighted down his barrel, and then pulled the gun in close, licked his thumb and wiped the front sight with the moisture. Taking aim again, the whistle blew and they let fire.

Boom! Boom! The muskets gave a thunderous roar and expelled a huge plume of smoke thanks to the little extra powder added by the vendor. When the smoke cleared, the taller boys' target was completely intact, not a single tear or hole. The shorter boys target was completely blown to shreds, even the hickory post was cut in half.

Everyone was whooping and hollering and running to slap him on the back. The Mr. Snead said he had never seen a fellow that young shoot that well. Tha was some mighty fine shooting.

"It will be a pleasure to give you the prize," and with that, the "expert" shooter walked off with a real live turkey as the prize. Both boys scrambled over to shorter boys' mother who was still standing by, and gave her the turkey.

After the excitement calmed down he looked at the taller boy and said, "I don't really shoot that well, did you shoot my target?"

The taller boy answered, "I just figured you could use a turkey more'n me."

Just then, the boys locked eyes, and right then, they knew their's would be a lasting friendship for the rest of their lives. The shorter boy said, "I don't even know your name, friend."

"It's Abe, Abe Lincoln, and it's a pleasure to meet ya. What name do yea be using?"

"Jefferson, Jefferson Davis. But friends call me Jeff. Thanks for your help," Jefferson said.

"Don't mention it, Jeff, just don't tell my momma," Abe said.

Just then the boys heard a loud yell and lots of commotion out toward the road. Apparently, a wheel had come off a buckboard wagon and the axle had a man trapped. Abe and Jeff both ran to help, each grabbing hold of the side of the wagon. They were lifting with all their might as were two older men but could not even budge the wagon with its heavy load. Suddenly, another young man about a year or two older than them came running over. Dirty from head to toe, he grabbed the wagon with Abe and Jeff and darn near hoisted it off the ground, raising it off both wheels. Abe looked at Jeff, blinking questioningly. Several others pitched in and helped drag the man out from under the axle. Fortunately, he was only cut up slightly and bruised. The boys looked at the older youth, astonished, as he lowered the wagon to the ground.

"Wow!" both boys exclaimed!

"How could you do that? Both of us together couldn't lift the wagon, and you lifted it all by yourself!"

The boy seemed to be in a big hurry to get away. Jeff called to him that there's nothing to be afraid of.

"What's your hurry?"

Then Abe said, "Friend, at least tell me your'n name before you run off."

The boy looked at Abe and Jeff and said, "My name is Arthur, but don't tell nobody."

And with that he ran as fast as he could back down the main street toward the Blacksmith work shed. Abe and Jeff stood looking at each other.

Finally, Jeff asked, "Did you ever see anything like that in all your born days?" Abe shook his head and said, "I never did see nobody that could pick up a wagon all by his self. He is almighty strong. My pappy is the strongest man I ever seen and he couldn't lift a wagon like that."

"He said his name is Arthur. I seen him working over at the Blacksmith's with his Pa shoeing horses.

I heard tell there was a strong man who lived around here, but I figured he was a grown man. Surely not someone just a few years older than me.

Abe imagined he should be in the fair doing a show.

"I bet people would come from miles around to see someone his age lift heavy stuff."

Jeff nodded, "I would'a paid a penny myself to see something like what I seen him do, if'n I had a penny. The boys laughed and started walking back down the street.

"I ain't seen your'n around these parts afore, you live here?" asked Abe.

"We used to live near here then my Pa moved us to Louisiana, explained Jeff. "That's where we live now. We come home cuz my Uncle Josh was killed when his horse kicked him in the head. We come home for his funeral. I expect we will be headed back to Louisiana after that. I sure wish I lived here again now."

"Why is that?" asked Abe.

"I have my first good friend and it's in a place I don't live n no more."

Abe smiled and said, "That's ok. I think we will be the only ones around that has a friend that lives across the country.

"Well, said Jeff, "Louisiana ain't quite across the country but I know what you mean. I didn't think about it like that. I like that."

"I hope we will always be friends," said Jeff.

"Of course, we will, and who knows, maybe we'll see each other again and have another shooting competition," brightened Abe.

"I sure hope so, I sure would like that."

They two boys then walked back toward the county fair. The wind started blowing just enough to pick up the dust and blow it in their faces. They stood there a moment.

Abe said, "I'll write yea a letter if'n you tell me where your'n house is. Maybe we can write each other about all our adventures until we meet again."

"I don't write so good, but I can get my mama to help. I think that is a grand idea!" With that they shook hands and said good-by. Abe watched and smiled again as Jeff took his turkey from his mom and turned toward Abe, and waved good-bye again. He looked at his mom and smiled, and said, "Mom, I really like that boy. I bet we could be good friends."

His mom smiled, "Jeff, you never know what the future holds for you. You just might meet him again and get your wish."

Of course, neither boy could know what the future had in store for them, yet they had already set the gears of history in motion. Each would have the weight of a nation resting on his shoulders.

Abe walked through town and before he knew it he was outside the blacksmith shop. He could see Arthur inside stoking the fire with the huge bellow. Abe stepped inside and stood watching Arthur for a minute. He didn't think Arthur's muscles were nearly large enough to lift the heavy load but he sure lifted it. He looked at Abe and asked, "What do you want?"

"I just wanted to say thank you again and to tell you I ain't never seen anything like that in all my life."

Arthur spat, "I told you to keep it to yourself. A thing like that gets around and people start treating you different like you got a sickness and was the devil."

"I guess you are right, friend, but it sure is a shame cause what you done was such a good thing. People should know you are a hero."

Arthur looked at Abe with fire in his eyes, "Don't you tell nobody. Just mind your business and leave me alone."

Abe knew when to quit. At that, he stuck out his hand and said, "You're right, friend. My name is Abe, Abe Lincoln. What's your given name, Arthur?"

"It's DeKay. Arthur DeKay. My pa is French and Irish and my ma is Native American. We moved here afore I was born. I like it here," Arthur told Abe.

"Where you from?"

Abe answered, "A small place called Knob Creek, just near Hodgenville, Kentucky. About a two-day trip from here. I always wanted to come to the county fair so my ma and pa brought me and my sister. She likes the cattle and spends all her time over there with my Pa. Abe said, "Is that your Pa pointing to the Blacksmith. Arthur said, "It sure is". He's the hardest working man I know. He keeps the horses moving and the wagons rolling. Well, "Abe said, I hope to see you again sometime. But I live near Hodgenville, Kentucky. About a two day ride from here. Hey, me and my pa have to travel a lot sometimes to go to different farms and repair all sorts of machinery. We might run into each other again sometime. They shook hands again and Arthur felt a jolt or shock. He could not explain the sensation, but it was real enough. Abe released his grip and asked, "are you alright?" Arthur said, sure I'm ok. Abe walked off saying I sure hope so.

Abe slowly fades back into 1864.

Abe is standing in the kitchen, remembering the years that had passed and reflecting on the letters he and Jeff had sent one another. How excited he would be anticipating the next letter every month or two. Their friendship continued to grow over the years. The two boys finally met again as men when they both entered politics. Abe just smiled remembering a simpler time.

"Abe, let's hammer this thing down," Jeff said, "I think this is the best we can do."

CHAPTER 8

JOE

Born in Petersburg, Joe played on the battlefields as a youngster. In the very hole on the battlefield, where so many hundreds of lives were lost, Joe would explore where the tunnel was blown up, creating the tremendous **Crater**. Now known as the "Battle of the Crater," Joe played atop the very cannons that were used during the war. They were the instruments that brought death and mutilation to thousands, destroying hundreds more lives and altering the course of untold many more. Joe's playground was the very cannons that abruptly ended so many family trees. If you are very quiet you can still hear the moans of those men who were physically torn apart and lay dying in the fields.

As a child in Petersburg, a simple walk through the woods would invariably turn into a great adventure. The siege of Petersburg was one of the longest battles during the civil war. Two different battles raged in Petersburg throughout the 1860 to 1865 war. The longest lasting over a year. On numerous occasions, Joe would find civil war bullets (called mini balls) fired from guns of both sides, embedded in the clay walls of the creeks. Joe's discoveries were bullets that were meant to kill many and may have. He found old musket parts and wagon wheels that carried the heavy cannons from battle to battle. Pieces of belt buckles with the emblem "CSA" on the front lie here and there, and his discovery of an old campsite, complete with a garbage dump from camps during civil war years.

The trash from the 1860s were now treasures of 1963. Joe unearthed triangular-shaped bottles with deformed glass, some brown, some purple, the corks within, having disintegrated long ago.

As a child, these finds were exciting but only for brief moments. Leaving most of those treasures where he found them, Joe continued to explore new areas, looking to play in other woods, and find new treasures.

Always fascinated with treasure hunting, and exploring new and oftentimes very dangerous areas, and things, Joe experienced something else unusual. Occasionally, especially when he touched or held a piece from the long ago past, he experienced "visions" of past events in history, and even sometimes of the future. Extraordinarily, sometimes, if he could "see" enough of a future event in his visions to know when it would take place, he found he could alter the occurrence or at least some part of the occurrence.

Joe never discussed these visions with anyone, not even his closest childhood friends or parents. He believed anyone he told would think he was crazy or odd. Much later, Joe came to understand these visions were some kind of extra sensory perception or something related. Joe also understood that scientists still thought the brain was capable of accomplishing amazing feats that we simply could not tap into. Throughout his teenage years, other unique abilities emerged. Joe walked or ran almost everywhere he went. In elementary and into high school, he learned he could run faster than everyone else. Soon, he forced himself to run at half his possible speed to appear normal. But he loved it. Joe ran all over town. He was not a Flash Gordon but could still run fast.

In high school, he was about 5'8" tall and weighed 130 pounds. A typical young man, he was not exceptionally muscular, with average looks. Oddly, Joe was abnormally strong for his age and build and could lift over four times his weight. He could easily win arm wrestling matches with grown men outweighing him by 150 to 200 pounds. But he dared not let out his secret. Trying his hand at a little weightlifting in school, he surprised himself at just how much weight he could lift. His friends encouraged him to compete with all the older boys.

He realized he had to be careful not to become the local freak. Joe's feats astonished the coach's, especially since most of them were after the kid who could make them the star coach. Not wanting the attention, Joe decided it would be safer if he withdrew from school sports.

One day, while in the gym by himself, he loaded up the barbell with 600 pounds of weight and focused his brain and all thought to the bar, then grabbed the bar in the center   with his right hand. He jerked the bar up and over his head in one smooth motion and held it for about 10 seconds before gently lowering it back to the floor. He surprised himself that he was not winded. And then, as he removed the weight from the bar, he noticed it was heavily bent. The weight was too much for the bar.

He had grown-up in a loving family environment but somehow felt out-of-place. He knew he possessed abilities that other people did not. His mom or dad never discussed anyone in the family ever having special abilities, so he figured it must be him only. He had real strength that he believed came from brain focus. He still had not measured just how much weight he could lift, push or pull, but he knew it was a lot. He never let others see him lift weight more than 200 pounds. He could also somehow tune the sensitivity of his hearing and listen and hear sounds from far away. If he were at a high school football game and tuned in on a couple sitting in the bleachers on the opposite side of the field, he could understand what they were saying. He could also tune out all the other noises. This ability often got him in trouble as he would end up knowing things he should not sometimes. Then he would be questioned as to how he knew, and he had to come up with a sufficient-enough answer. He also had a photographic memory that allowed him to picture a scene in his mind and he could recall the style and color of clothes that every classmate was wearing yesterday and the day before and if he thought hard enough the day before that. He had a lot of fun using this ability.

When he arrived home that night, he walked over to his mom's station wagon on the way into the house. He grabbed the back bumper and lifted the car to his knees. He then walked around to the front of the car and lifted the front tires clear off the ground with ease.

"Stop that!" hollered his mother from the window, "You'll hurt yourself!"

Little did she know (he thought) what he had just accomplished or what she had just witnessed. Climbing was yet another unique ability Joe discovered.

He could run and jump up on a building, deftly finding small places to grab hold and scale the side. Joe could scramble up most buildings and get on the roof before other people got out of their car. He realized he had tremendous strength in the tips of his fingers and in his hands as well. After high school, Joe held a multitude of different jobs including, house construction, building custom kitchen cabinets, painting and restoring houses, church steeples, towers, smokestacks and bridges. For some reason, he felt at ease when he was outside and high up in the air. Most people either could not or would not do these jobs, fearful of the danger. But not Joe. Because these jobs required men of strength, Joe was always looking forward to the next highest, most dangerous job. His main problem was he found that after mastering a job and learning everything he could, after a couple of years he became bored easily and would begin looking for his next challenge. A passionate learner from childhood, he was always an avid reader and read every "How To" Book printed. Joe devoured books on aviation, engineering, motorcycle repair, scuba diving, woodworking, and politics.

But he also had an appetite for adventure and enjoyed novels on treasure hunting, and sunken ships. He often joked about being stranded in a bookstore with nothing to do but read. As he grew older, he took courses and learned how to fly small aircraft including helicopters. He obtained his Private Pilot License at the age of 16. Afterwards, he learned to skydive, scuba dive, water ski, and snow ski, and he loved Bungee Jumping and welding. He not only became proficient at a task, but would do his best to master everything he attempted. His Karate and Ju-Jitsu instructors spoke highly of his abilities and he even became a police officer for several years and was rapidly promoted to investigator. Quick to make friends, Joe believed in the power of friendship and having friends for life. He always pulled for the underdog and took up for those that were bullied or ridiculed. This is probably what made him successful as a cop.

When he was 19, his parents were killed in a plane crash. He inherited a sizable amount of money and made several sound investments that would pay off handsomely a few years later.

Always sensible, he never spent excessively, and never let on that he had much money. But Joe truly enjoyed providing help to others in need whenever he could. Joe was a man of integrity. He believed that you should live on the right side of things and do what was best. Now this did not always agree with the letter of the law. The law was written years ago when it suited that time and the way people lived. The law should be under constant change to keep current and serve the people of this time and place.

Joe was quick to point out a defective or antiquated law, and then attempt to get it changed or repealed. On the other hand, if there was a need for a law to be enacted, he worked with the politicians to get it passed into law for the safety of the public. Shortly after his parents died, Joe lost himself for a time. He spent his days jumping off the New River Gorge Bridge in West Va. with a parachute or bungee cord or he could be found Jumping off Arches in Park City, Utah. He became an adrenaline junkie and loved fast, high, and dangerous. But, at the end of the day he would return to his painting job and his old friend John. John tried to convince Joe to slow down and do something relaxing like fishing for a change. One day John and Joe went fishing in the Newport News Harbor in Virginia. John really enjoyed fishing and was very good at it. He said the "Crappie" were running and they were good to eat. So they anchored in the harbor close to a pipe that was near the middle and started fishing. We were catching Crappie two at a time and rapidly filling the cooler with nice size fish. About an hour later, Joe looked at the pipe and noticed it was about 50 feet farther away than when they anchored. John said the anchor must have got loose. He reached over and grabbed the anchor line and tugged. It was nice and tight on the bottom. Suddenly, the water started churning and bubbling and shooting up in the air. John yelled "Sea Monster" and started the boat and took off. Joe hollered, "let me get the anchor in the boat" and John yelled back, the hell with the anchor!

Just about that same time they both saw the sea monster. It was a Navy submarine coming up. What they thought was a pipe had been their periscope. They figured the Navy had been watching them fish and got a great laugh.

CHAPTER 9

JOE'S VISION

Joe still laid there unconscious. John was getting worried that they would get caught. He kept calling for Joe but when he did not get an answer, he figured Joe was down in the tunnel, out of earshot.

Joe was unconscious but dreaming. In Joe's dream, he was seeing General Lee in the mansion arguing with several other high-ranking Confederate Officers. He could barely hear their conversation but could understand the General discussing the "tunnel" and making it secure in the event a hasty escape to the river was necessary. The smell of the stale air in the brick was strong and he could smell the scent of black powder smoke mixed with the stale air.

The arch that he crawled through now appeared to disappear. Instead, Joe saw a long tunnel, ten feet high with "miners" timber and brick supporting the walls and ceiling. Fifteen feet wide and square, the tunnel was busy with several men walking around inside, dressed in confederate uniforms and hats. Several cannons, stacks of cannon balls, wooden crates of rifles and lots of large brown bottles filled with a clear liquid lined the walls. Two of the soldiers were ordered to stack the heaviest crates in a special room as well as those marked "UCSA". Some crates containing rifles also had the special designation on them.

Clarence Roberts and Jeremy Stiles were trusted solders who hoped to one day become members of an elite team they had heard about.

They spent most of their time loading or unloading crates for delivery elsewhere. This assignment would be their first test to measure their ability to keep secrets. Jeremy had been given a written order of their assignment and each man was given a gold twenty-dollar double eagle as special compensation. These crates contained the newest .44 caliber "Henry" repeating rifles and plenty of ammunition. These weapons replaced the popular Springfield rifles and could help win the war. The men recruited eight other soldiers to help carry the crates from the supply wagons through the basement and into the tunnel, stacking some against the far wall and others into the corner room. Some crates were marked "High Explosives" "Do Not Drop" "Store in a Dry Cool Place" while others were taken through the tunnel to a waiting boat. His understanding was that those crates would eventually be loaded on a train bound for Richmond.

One of the solders named Stephen Booth kept complaining of having diarrhea, a common ailment, and would disappear down the tunnel for fifteen to twenty minutes, and then would be back carrying more supplies. Booth always seemed to be carrying the boxes of explosives, both dynamite and nitroglycerin. Jeremy had an uneasy feeling about Stephen but maybe it was simply a notion because everything else was running perfectly.

The crates in the corner room were stacked into triple stacks, four high, very neatly, with all writing visible. Additional crates of guns were stacked against the back wall of the room. Other crates of very heavy duty wood, were banded in cast iron supports and marked "H. L. Hunley." They were built to hold much heavier cargo, he observed. In the front of each crate was a single hole, the shape of a very large skeleton key. He wished he knew the contents as he could tell that the contents must be very important.

One of the soldiers had a blood-soaked bandage wrapped around his left arm and was complaining about the possibility of losing it. As Joe watched, he could see the soldiers' breath as they exhaled, figuring it must be winter.

Every time they walked and stepped hard, dust rose from the dirt floor. There were many different smells in the air, oil lamps and gun powder, and then the smell of wood and dirt.

Every once in a while, he thought he caught the scent of the river in the air. The men coughed and cursed the cold and their hunger.

"When do you think the boat will be here," asked Stephen?

Another soldier answered, "Quit yer bellyaching. I heard them say in about an hour."

"So, we should be able to get everything secured before dawn maybe?" asked Clarence?

Jeremy answered, "I think you will be back in your bed before 5:00 if we keep at it."

Then he asked, "Why do you think this little room over here in this odd corner of the main hall is built like a fortress? Some of the heaviest timber and metal I ever seen is on the walls and it looks like a marble floor. All this, and no door? People do some strange things. Git Adam and Roy to come down and help with the heavy stuff."

Both young and muscular, and a little stupid, it would probably take most of the night to get the supplies off the wagons and loaded in here. Jeremy had a bandaged arm from a bayonet stab during a battle several days ago. He reached in a pocket and pulled out the written order one more time to be sure he knew it by heart. He also dumped the contents of a small dirty cloth bag containing the coin into his hand. He again read the order and shook his head as if bewildered. Just then, he put tobacco inside a cigarette paper, and reached in his pocket, pulled out a match, struck it, inhaled, and coughed twice. He then rolled the coin around in his hand and rubbed the engraving on one side. It was then that he noticed what appeared to be initials on the bottom of the worn paper faded from being folded and read many times. Joe struggled to make out the initials at the bottom of the paper; the two letters looked to be the initials "A.L.".

Joe finally snapped to it, woke up, and yelled for John, who came running. "Are you alright? I was getting really worried."

John helped Joe get out of the tunnel and replace the brick. "We need to stay out of there," cautioned John to Joe.

"You haven't seen what I saw in there..."

"Well, let's get back to work," said John, "You can dream later...I would really like to keep my job for a while longer.

CHAPTER 10

BACK TO WORK

  The next morning, Joe was brimming with excitement thinking about what he saw. He could not wait to get to work so he could remove some brick and really get a good look in that hole. He was thinking how he would walk around the building to see if he could figure out if it was one room, or multiple rooms that were concealed in the brick. But first, he had something else to do. There was something that kept nagging at the back of his mind. And he was compelled to figure it out.

  Before he left for work, he went up into his attic where he kept everything of his parents in sealed containers. He had never met his great grandfather, but his mother and grandmother spoke of his exploits often. Apparently, he had been an adventurer that had many different experiences throughout his life. Joe seemed to remember his mother reading some old letters that his great grandfather had written to his great grandmother during the civil war. From what he knew, his grandfather seemed like an extraordinary person. He recalled hearing his mother reading about a long trip or adventure his grandfather had gone on and something about a tunnel collapse. Surely it was not the same tunnel. Inside a container, he found the small oak box he was looking for and opened it.

  Several letters and some ribbons lie in the box along with five multi-colored medals. Joe picked up the letters to read them. One described the different countryside he was seeing for the first time in detail and there were tales about the war and how horrible it was.

Then he read the letter he was looking for. It read: it was the worst tragedy I ever witnessed.

The train exploded and the sounds of men and women screaming could be heard just over the cries of pain from the horses as if they knew death had arrived. The train cars fell into the deepest part of the river, whole and exploded train cars, and bodies of people. The main two cars that fell into the river carried the salvation for the Union; salvation that shined bright. Folding up the letter, Joe now knew exactly what he had to do.

Joe and John got to work early before anyone else got there so they could spend some time without interruption. Joe shined the flashlight into the hole.

"I can barely see, but it looks like it goes a good twenty feet back. I can see something, I just can't tell what it is. Then John took the light and looked for himself. It looks like there is another room in there.

"I think it is pretty long, but I can't tell exactly. Let's go ahead and put the brick back in. We need to get back to work."

Joe replaced the brick and put some mortar caulking around the joints and went back to work.

"Man," he thought, "How am I supposed to work until I know what is in there?

"Whatever is in there, if anything, has been there for a long time, John said, impatiently. "It can wait a little longer."

Joe was disappointed but as usual, John was right. The suspense was killing him but Joe would just have to wait. Besides, there may be nothing more than dirt and mold in there. The shiny gold looking stuff may have been part of the dream from when he fell. Maybe it had been a root cellar where they used to store vegetables during the hot summer months.

Even so, Joe could not help but let his imagination run wild. So, they went back to work sandblasting, scraping, and dusting.

CHAPTER 11

MARCH 1863 – THE PROTECTORS

Created in 1862, in total secret, by two great men who had an idea for assuring the financial stability of a nation prior to the end of the Civil War, the "Protectors" was the brainchild of Colonel Arthur B. DeKay. Colonel DeKay was a man of great foresight who predicted that presidents and visiting dignitaries might need bodyguards. There were people whose opinions and views on worldly comforts differed and could be interpreted as threats. He also knew that certain tasks that had to be completed could only be done by trusted individuals. That way the top brass could always have "Plausible Deniability" if things went badly.

There was a very tight circle of people who understood the need for these hand selected men and women. The man in charge was also a spit and polish, no nonsense, get the job done kind of man. Everyone simply called him "Colonel".

Although he had worn just about every rank the Army issued, he was now retired and had been specially selected as the leader of the protectors. The "Colonel" was Arthur B. DeKay himself. He continued to wear his Army hat with the Colonel designation on the front. Proud of his rank, he displayed it with honor and never ever allowed anyone to bring discredit to the designation. At 6'2" and 225 pounds, he was no slouch. He was handsome but rugged, with a deep commanding voice. Son of a French/Irish father and a Native

American mother, he could out drink, out fight, and out cuss most men alive.

His father had also spent most of his life doing blacksmith work and anything he did, he did very well, and his business was no different. It was an honorable profession but extremely hot and physically difficult. Arthur was always looking for better ways to get something done. He was usually thinking three steps ahead of everyone else, a trait that had nearly gotten him into serious trouble plenty of times. He had the unique ability to track and anticipate the movements of anything moving on two or four legs. A skill he learned from his mother and used well. Colonel DeKay had fists the size of frying pans and used them often. As a young man, he realized that he possessed certain "special abilities" that he would have to keep concealed or contained from everyday use. Knowing if he did not, he would be placed among the ranks of freaks or simply shunned by everyday people. Two of his greatest abilities were physical strength and photographic memory. He could remember everything he read, smelled, tasted, touched, observed, or heard. So far, his strength had no match, but he called upon it only when needed and without public display. He also possessed a keen hearing ability. Fortunately, he could turn it on and off as needed. Colonel DeKay had also received training in Europe, specifically Japan, India, and Australia, as his once blacksmith father ended up working with a man named Colt. He would forge new metals that created firearms never seen. Then together they would travel and sell them to nations that wanted to see and own the best firearm available by the standards of the day.

As a young boy, Arthur DeKay starved for knowledge, always learning new skills and abilities along with many languages during their travels. He mastered the firearm quickly and remained a master shooter. Now, as an adult, Colonel DeKay knew that the country needed specially- trained and highly-skilled individuals to perform certain tasks and duties that politicians did not speak about at parties, and that government officials denied knowledge of, but totally supported. Later, both the Northern and Southern governments would continue to invest in the training of these men and women. They had been assembled from both sides of the country when lines were being drawn.

Each man and woman were true patriots and, loved and would die, for the United States of America. They all wanted a united country.

When they were not fighting others for God and country, they were fighting each other to keep their skills sharp. They never fought over politics or passion, and never caused each other any permanent injury as they were a team with one goal in mind, success for the country.

For the most part, all personal feelings about the war and the politics were tucked away deep inside. But on rare occasions, those personal feelings would rear up, and would have to be dealt with.

The protectors were eight in number, for no particular reason other than that was the number the "Colonel" knew he could train, supervise, and control at a time. Five men and three women comprised the team deemed necessary for most missions. Two were still in training, and six were trained and ready. There was no exact set time for the training period, but somehow the Colonel always seemed to know when they were ready. When the instructors assured him that they were all ready for the mission, he always interviewed each person for the job himself. Now mind you, the interview might take place after a brawl at the local saloon or at a tavern, or at some other location where a near-death event occurred and where the person's skills could be observed firsthand by the Colonel.

Each person that was selected for training and to ultimately become a team member, possessed a special ability or skill that made him or her unique. Each were required to pledge to never use the skill unless directed by Colonel DeKay to do so. The training they received from the "Colonel" fine-tuned their skills. They were taught lessons in etiquette, law, and living off the land. The members were taught skills of how to improvise and make use of whatever was at their disposal to save themselves and others. Each completed a strict physical regime every morning and evening to maintain their top form and strength.

None of the trainees had any living relatives nor significant others. Colonel DeKay had realized a long time ago that a person without strings and potential heartache was easier to train, lacking the normal distractions that inadvertently came with relationships and family. These luxuries could wait until they retired or they could simply quit to have a relationship.

The gender numbers were simply based on the need for brute strength, more often than not. Vigilance and being observant were critical; the "Colonel" said he would teach them to have eyes in the back of their head.

The art of listening, was a key part of learning this skill, even when the noise in a room was loud, he taught them how to pick out certain sounds and vibrations and zero in on those. Sometimes, you knew when a person was behind you or watching you from a distance because of a strange feeling. He taught them how to pay attention to that feeling and how to hone it because it was rarely misinterpreted, and it could easily save their lives.

CHAPTER 12

PROTECTOR TRAINING

The "Protectors" trained together at a secret location in South Carolina known only to Colonel DeKay and his small group of instructors. It was affectionately referred to by the recruits as "Camp Satan," named for their no-nonsense attitude toward their mission and lack of personality among the ranks of the instructors. Four top-notch "killer" instructors worked with the "Protectors" day and night to enhance their secret skills and abilities, each possessing their own strengths. The instructors pushed the trainees to the point of exhaustion, and then pushed harder. They made sure when they told the "Colonel" a recruit was ready for service; the recruit had mastered their lessons in every way. They trained, ate, played, and slept within reach of each other every day. There was no quitting or dropping out. They had little contact with the outside world except during monthly breaks for re-supply and even those were limited to no more than three going into the same town at a time. They always remained very conscious of their mission and need for secrecy.

To the untrained eye these particular men and women, these "Protectors", seemed like very ordinary people. Very few knew that they were a culmination of the most highly trained and specially outfitted men and women in America. They were the forerunners of the Secret Service, FBI, Rangers, Seals and CIA in that they were hired to perform specialized duties for the President of the United States of America. That was where the similarities ended.

These men and women also possessed special skills and abilities unique to certain tasks that they may be called upon to perform. In addition to all other learned skills and abilities, each was trained in a new "lethal" Asian art mastered in the Orient by none other than the "Colonel" himself. He trained each instructor until they mastered the skill and could teach it each student. This was the art quickly and quietly taking a life using their bare hands and fingers with only slight movements and pressure points. They could slip into a room completely undetected as quiet as a snake, kill the intended target(s), yet never disturb someone sleeping beside them, and then slip out again. Every one of them could shoot you in the eye at 30 yards. The women could seduce a man into leaning on a blade and dying, if she desired. Every one of them could punch with lightning speed, their victim falling dead before they knew they had been hit. Running was the easiest activity; they could run and jump on a horse. Climbing up walls or slipping up porch posts to the roof was quick and simple. Once there, the trained killers could turn and shoot someone in the street before that person ever knew what was happening. They were instructed how to charm their way through the gates of hell when needed and then slip back out before Satan ever knew they had stopped by. The men were just as adept at seduction and could charm a rattlesnake to bite itself. This exclusive group of men and women knew the meaning of Honor, Integrity, Ethics, Morals, Principles and Values, and practiced them. They were words they chose to live by. These were the most trusted individuals, bar none. They were entrusted with closely-guarded national secrets until their death, and they would keep them. Colonel DeKay held all these traits himself and demanded them of everyone he considered worthy of being called an American. The "Colonel" also has the dubious distinction of having two very close friends: Presidents Lincoln and Davis.

A deeply secret meeting was held to work out the specifics of the "mission" as it was called. Presidents Lincoln and Davis had called in great favors, made promises, offered future positions in government, and made death demands based on treason to obtain the goals of the "mission". As Director of the U.S. Treasury, Salmon

Chase had assured President Lincoln that he had the full resources of the treasury department to make things happen.

After all, the treasury held gold deposits from all over the North and South. As they explained the mission to Colonel DeKay, he considered his team and if they were ready for a mission of this magnitude. It entailed traveling for about eight months under harsh conditions. Colonel DeKay accepted this mission because he respected both men, and he believed what they were attempting to accomplish. They had forged a lifelong friendship and he would do everything in his power and use every skill he had to successfully complete this mission.

CHAPTER 13

THE MISSION

The mission: Secretly collect gold from every federally owned and operated mint in the United States to include California, Nevada, Arizona, Colorado, Utah, South Dakota, Philadelphia, Louisiana, and Georgia. Next, they would transport it safely to a secret location in Petersburg, Virginia where half would be unloaded in Petersburg to be sent later to Richmond, Va., the Confederate Capital. The other half would be loaded on a train and sent to Washington, DC, to another secret location there. The two locations for deposit were known only to the Presidents and Colonel DeKay. Their journey was made even more difficult with the fear of word getting out about their trained group. If the curious and the greedy learned about them, they would be upon them without delay.

Throughout the trip, they would be met for exchanges at predetermined checkpoints, the location of which was known only to their commander. Their horses would be exchanged for fresh mounts, and their supplies, replenished. At these checkpoints, additional pack mules and loaded wagons would be added. The pack mules could carry far heavier loads of supplies than ordinary horses. The heavy- duty wagons were built especially for carrying these heavy crates and were constructed of heavier iron with slightly wider wheels than normal to traverse the mud and terrain of the rugged countryside.

Special "floaters" were added to help in crossing wide expanses of water. Having been a blacksmith, the Colonel designed and oversaw the construction of these wagons for strength, because at each checkpoint, their load increased substantially. Before they reached their destination, they would have accumulated some twelve wagons.

Two carried supplies and 10 would carry the gold. The horses and mules were well fed and watered and always groomed at the close of the day. All tack was made of the finest leather and iron available. The brass buckles were smooth, shiny and new. Colonel DeKay could not wait for the brass to dull so it would not reflect in the sunlight.

The route they took was seldom used by families and most travelers because it was far more difficult than the normal route. However, this route would provide them with some invisibility they could maintain through most of the trip, knowing that if they could not be seen, they would be left alone. He also knew that because of the size of the group, they would be hard to miss by even the most blind Indian scouts.

CHAPTER 14

AUGUST 1863 – TIME TO GO

"Mount Up!"

Colonel DeKay bellowed at first light. He never wasted any time of the day that he could use to his advantage. He loved the early morning; the air, crisp and cool, smelled new. His senses were at their peak at this time of day and in its clarity, he could sense trouble brewing from far away when the air had just a hint of chill and felt wafer thin on his skin. Even Colonel DeKay had no exact knowledge of the ultimate use of the gold. He only knew that it was to be used in an unprecedented way to restore the country. His orders were simple and the map he was provided, very basic. The routes had been outlined with dates and the name of each town, city, or area when and where he should be and the first name of their contact. Wait no longer than one day for contact then improvise and move on. His orders were: Head due West, where he'd be met in three days and given fresh supplies, cargo, and directions. Protect the shipment and let nothing stand in your way. Simple enough. Sure.

Each protector was outfitted with new, yet untested in the field, .44 Caliber Henry repeating rifles. These were the finest repeating rifles built in the country. The detail also carried Sharps carbines which were considered the long-range sniper weapon of the era and 4 Gatlin guns which were mounted on individual wagons and placed at strategic points and could literally spray hundreds of bullets at rapid speed to kill en mass.

On the day of departure, they left a small town in South Carolina riding on a specially outfitted train created just for them, their horses, and supplies. The time spent riding was put to good use, offering them the ability to complete training, honing those newly-acquired skills. Shooting and tracking animals for food were among the first used skills, and Colonel DeKay observed quickly that the training had paid off. Routes were worked and reworked by his team attempting to offer them the shortest distance with the fewest obstructions known at the time. As long as they were at the checkpoints on time was all that mattered. They would always need fresh water and food, and although their map showed them the basic route to head, they still had to improvise for water and changes in landscape.

Strategies were troubleshot over and over. This was sure to be an incredible journey, one that would test the mental and physical metal of each one of them. South Carolina was full of swamps, rivers, streams, and creeks. Thick woods provided cover for those hunting and the game source was plentiful. Deer, wild hogs, rabbit, and squirrel topped the list of daily foods. They would catch the occasional alligator for different meat. The main preoccupation of the day and nights became apparent in the hot summer month of August in South Carolina: swatting flies and slapping biting mosquitoes. There was also no short supply of venomous creatures around. These however helped to keep their shooting instincts intact along the way. Also, for those with such an appetite, the snakes made for a quick, easy meal.

Crossing into Tennessee, they met some Cherokee Indians on their own hunting expedition and offered a trade of sugar for skins. This meeting went very well as Colonel DeKay was proficient in the language of the Cherokee. Some of these Cherokee spoke very broken English, but enough to get by. They also traded information on good water ahead for both. This meeting ended on a good note with wishes of good hunting and long lives for all. Some meetings with other tribes would not go as well.

Whenever hostile Indians came close the protectors would fire off a few rounds and they would scatter and disappear just as fast as they had shown up.

They were little more than a nuisance for the most part. However, Colonel DeKay seized every opportunity he could to forge a new relationship knowing that in this forbidden country, a person in need could always use a friend.

Whenever they approached an encampment of seemingly friendly Indians, he would always tend to their sick as best he could and provide them some sugar and regale them with drink and food and tall tales of glorious expeditions. He always seemed to amuse the Indians as best he could communicate. He always said that there were only slight differences in the Indian languages. You simply had to listen carefully, know a little French, Spanish, and Latin, and you'd be able to understand the rest by hand gestures and facial expression.

Along the trail, they made many friendships and word spread quickly that this group should be left alone. Other expeditions would not be so fortunate. When they did cross a familiar stretch of road, they always saw the remnants of some families' dreams spread out along the road where either the Indians had killed the owners and ransacked their belongings, or the owners' mules or horses had died and they attempted to carry the load as far as they could themselves before the weight overcame them. Many would die of exhaustion and starvation.

This journey would take them through some of the most rugged terrain in the country.

Much of the landscapes and terrain they encountered, few white men had ever laid eyes on. And yet still, most people had never seen.   Places like the Rocky Mountains, the Grand   Canyon, Yellowstone,   or   the   rolling   hills   of   Wyoming   challenged and amazed them.   They would see strange sites like   the   Devils Tower, in Wyoming and in the East, into and through the Black Hills of South Dakota into what would later became known as Deadwood, famously renowned for the death of Wild Bill Hickok. Deadwood was also a place of murder for fun, greed, hire, and to settle a debt; it also was on their list of places to stop. Gold had been discovered in the Black Hills all around Deadwood where it became a mecca of population explosion where every person had dreams and hopes.

Whether they aimed to discover a fortune in gold or to start a prosperous business selling guns and ammunition, hardware and supplies, prostitutes, tobacco, liquor, gambling, or other popular items of the day.

Some of the landscape appeared unholy but beautiful in its own way, such as the Badlands in South Dakota, an awesome sight but as harsh as any on earth and in nature. They would travel through the lush fields of Nebraska and into the green grasses of Kentucky, cross the Blue Ridge Mountains into Virginia and continue to head

East. As it turned out, the most difficult part of this epic journey was the weather. They endured long stretches of drought only to be immediately replaced by weeks of rain and vicious thunderstorms.

At each mine, they were not only expected but their shipment was packed, crated, and waiting for them. Colonel DeKay simply had to sign for the load. The director of the mint usually came out and introduced himself to the "Colonel". All but one had said, "I sure hope you guys know what you're doing". The "Colonel's" reply was always the same, "We can only have faith in God to see us through."

Their route caused them to "steer clear" of most towns, an intentional plan that the "Colonel" insisted upon. His rational was simple, every town had plenty of down and out thugs waiting to seize an opportunity for easy money. Most thugs were criminals but not stupid. Even they would question why so many people were riding with so many wagons. These wagons were not the normal traveling type. Anyone could see these were custom built, heavy duty load carrying wagons. The thugs of the day would want to know what was so heavy.

They broke a wheel hub and had to stop just outside the city limits of what is now known as Tombstone, Arizona. At the time, it was a small settlement of about eighty people located in Pima County, now known as Cochise County. This area was a dangerous place full of crooks, thugs, and vagabonds of every sort. They stopped off here to get a drink of whiskey and see what card games they could cheat. The "Colonel" decided he would break his own rule and have everyone go into town to at least get a bath. They could go in shifts.

CHAPTER 15

ROSIE B

"I need two volunteers to go into town and get supplies for the week, Lindsey and Blake. You two, go get ready to head out. Here is the list, the "Colonel" said, "Head over to the Macintosh Mercantile and give Mr. Macintosh this list. He will get it together and put it on my account. Hurry back."

Lindsey Berry was 25 years old and very strong for a woman.

She was born shortly after her Irish immigrant parents arrived in America. She was pretty, with a pale white color and satin smooth skin that most women would die for. Her blazing red hair, framed her green eyes, the color of emeralds, and her body was designed for enticing men no matter their religion or marital status. She was small in stature, about 5'5" but seemed taller when she wore her boots. She ran away from home at 18 when her father caught her and a ranch hand in the barn in compromising positions. Both were barely clothed and very much enjoying the pleasures that a sensuous touch could bring. She knew that her father would pretend to get over what happened, but she also knew she would never be able to stop having sexual fun now that she had been given a taste. She did not want to bring further embarrassment to him or her mom, so she left. She sent an occasional letter and money to her mom just to let her know she was well.

Blake Smith was 28 years old and had been captured by the Crow Indians near Belle Fourche South Dakota. The wagon train his parents were traveling with was raided and everyone killed. A band of renegade Crow Indians were responsible for the raid as the regular Crow were very peaceful. Blake was found in the cradle by a mother of one of the raiders and taken home. When he became a young warrior, he was given the Indian name that translated to "Little Mule Deer" because he could chase down most prey with his deer- quick running. She raised him until her death when he was 16 years old. By this time, he had learned all the Indian survival techniques such as tracking, stalking and killing prey, creating fire, and shooting an arrow as straight as any could. A plain but nice looking fellow, Blake had dark black hair and brown eyes. He was 6' tall and very slender. He could run as fast as a jackrabbit but never ran from a fight. His most outstanding feature was his thick bushy mustache.

Tired of riding on horseback, Blake and Lindsey drove the supply wagon into town. They were followed by the Colonel and Henry who rode straight to the bath house to get clean. Lindsey and Blake parked the wagon out front of the Mercantile. They walked into The Macintosh Mercantile, and Blake gave Mr. Macintosh the list. Mr. Macintosh said he would get everything loaded and ready and that it would take about 35 to 45 minutes. They could look around for a bit and come back and Lindsey had already spotted where she wanted to go. Directly across the street was a saloon called the Rosy B. owned and operated by big Rose Butler. Rose was a large woman that loved the affections of a man and enjoyed drinking just about as much. She could drink most men under the table and had gained quite a reputation for taking advantage of them after getting them completely drunk. Oh, she would take their money "honestly" by giving them a "feel" for a price which they were glad to pay in such a state of inebriation. She always carried a knife hidden from view and could use it if someone decided they wanted more than she wanted to give them.

In walked the two as though they had been there before. At seeing them, Big Rose jumped up and ran over and grabbed Lindsey in a big hug saying, "Lindsey! Where have you been? What's it been? 5 or 6 years? You know every time I see you I think you get prettier!

Maybe I just get older or need glasses. You know if I did not have such a likin' for men, I just might try you on for size!" Rose teased.

Lindsey said, "Well If I didn't have such a likin' for men myself, I just might oblige you. Men sure are a lot of trouble but I keep getting an itch that only they can scratch."

"HAW, HAW, HAW! I know what you mean," Rose said.

"I itch all the time," laughed Rose. "What brought you two into town?"

We had to get supplies from the mercantile so we're just killing some time and thought we might as well make sure you are still alive."

"Very funny. You know I'm for squeezing, not killing."

Lindsey said, "I'm teasing you of course. You have quite a reputation for being able to give better than you get."

At that, Rose laughed and said, "It would take a mighty big fellow to get the best of me. But you know, I AM getting older."

Three sodbusters had been playing cards at a table close to the bar and overheard the conversation between Rose and Lindsey. A particularly mean looking guy stood up and walked over to Lindsey and Rose and smiled through his grimy, yellow teeth.

He turned to Lindsey, "Why, darlin', you are the prettiest little girl I seen around here afore. How 'bout you and me going upstairs and get to know each other better?"

Blake, watching from across the room, spit a mouthful of beer and laughed. He could tell what was coming soon. But he also remembered what the Colonel told them. Just then he heard Lindsey say in her absolute best, most sarcastic voice, "Why honey that's the best offer I've had all day. And, from such a refined specimen of human carnage. I can barely resist such temptation. But, I find that I must sir. I am currently unable to indulge in the pleasures of another."

With that, the sodbuster stood close to Lindsey and said, "I ain't exactly sure of what you just said but I don't like the way it sounded. I just might have to spank you when I get you upstairs."

"Well, handsome, as divine as all that sounds, again, I am going to have to resist."

The sodbuster said, my name is Tate Larson, and this here is my brother, Sam. I don't appreciate those words you keep saying."

Sam was seated at a table with another sodbuster and told Tate, show her what you got Tate. Rose looked at Lindsey and said, "You got this? I have other customers."

Lindsey nodded affirmative and Rose walked away. Tate reached out and grabbed her arm and started to pull her toward the stairs. Lindsey grabbed his hand and turned it over and twisted it behind his back in one swift movement. She started to apply a little pressure which was very painful for him, and said, "Now I was trying to be nice and all, and now you done gone and ruined my mood."

With that, she applied more pressure, and he doubled over.

She took him to the floor easily so as not to hurt him, so fast he had no idea what happened. Even still, he cried out in pain and told her to let him go before he had to smack her around and teach her a lesson she would not forget. She applied a smidgen more pressure and he yelled for her to stop. The other two sodbusters at the table stood up and yelled for her to let him go!

Just then, Blake walked over and told them to sit down, she had it under control and was just playing with their friend. One of the two asked, "Who the hell you speaking to half-breed?" Get the fuck out of here before I have to throw you out on your face. Before he could move, Blake slapped him on the side of his face so hard he was knocked out and his buddy caught him before he hit the floor. Blake said we came in here to get a drink and did not want any trouble.

Lindsey pulled Tate back toward his table and sat him down next to his friend. Now I am willing to let you go, but when I do I don't expect you to do anything but sit here and finish your drink.

Nobody is hurt so enjoy the rest of your day. She then released his hand and he yelled about how she tried to break it off. As Lindsey turned and walked away, Tate jumped up and drew his gun and in the same instant Blake pulled and threw his knife and it struck Tate in his gun hand.

He dropped the gun and let out another yell. Blake walked over to Tate and jerked the knife out of his hand prompting a even louder yell from Tate.

Blake placed the knife back into the scabbard and looked at Tate and said, "Today is your lucky day."

"Are you crazy? How could today be my lucky day?"

Blake looked at Tate and smiled, and said, "I was aiming for your heart."

With that, Tate closed his eyes and sat back down. Lindsey and Blake walked over to the bar and ordered two whiskeys'. After a couple of drinks, Lindsey decided to give Rosie a hug and go get their supplies. As Lindsey stepped out front of the bar, she heard, then felt a gunshot behind her. She whirled around just in time to see Tate and his grimy grin, now a laugh, looking back at her holding his still smoking gun. Lindsey was shot clean through her left arm. She whipped out her 45 colt and shot Tate right between the eyes. He was dead before he hit the floor. Sometimes as much as you tried to mind your own business and stay out of trouble, trouble still manages to find you. Blake grabbed a towel and wrapped her arm to stop the bleeding.

"That man really wanted to die today." "Yes, he did."

Blake wrapped the towel carefully around her arm and tucked the loose end.

"That looks nice. Why are you so good to me?" Blake said, Because I love you."

They looked each other in the eyes. They stared long for a very uncomfortable moment, and then burst into laughter.

Later, they got their bath and picked·up the wagon and saw the Colonel and Henry coming out of a cigar shop. The Colonel asked Blake if he or Henry had missed anything exciting.

"Not at all," Blake said, "Seems to be a quiet little town."

They rode together during the trip back to camp. When they arrived, and were fixing the wheel hub, when the "Colonel" came up behind Blake and said, "Oh, by the way, Lindsey, what happened to your arm?"

Blake coughed and turned away from Lindsey, "Well," she said, "I had a disagreement with a slacker in the bar and he thought his knife and gun could impress me, but we left."

The "Colonel" looked at her and said, "Well, as long as nobody died, everybody should be alright."

On the return trip across what is now known as the Standing Rock Native American Reservation which covers part of North and South Dakota. It is inhabited by ethnic Hunkpapa and Sihasapa bands of Lakota Oyate as well as Hunkpatina Dakota. The group met with a small band of Sioux that were seemingly friendly. While conversing with the leader who called himself "Rising Moon, the "Colonel" kept picking up on body language and other small ques from the leader and two of his other warriors that troubled him. The 'Colonel" then asked Parker Reynolds who was sitting close by to "Make Some Tea". This was a code that meant "Trouble," be alert! Rising Moon must have sensed something because he and his warriors jumped up and he leveled his rifle at the "Colonel" and demanded their supplies and firearms. Little did Rising Moon know that his other five warriors had been put to sleep and tied up. The "Colonel" raised his hands and told Rising Moon that there was no need for all this. They would gladly share their food and supplies with the warriors. Rising Moon yelled at the "Colonel" to stop telling lies! All white men lied and destroyed the land and animals for pleasure. All they ever did was take and ruin everything in their path. The "Colonel" started to speak and Rising Moon yelled for him to shut up and reared back with his rifle to strike the "Colonel" across the face. Just then Brana, Tasha, Thomas, and

Axle came up behind the three warriors and assisted them in laying down and going to sleep. All eight were tied and would sleep until morning. Morning came and the warriors awoke questioning what had happened to them. The "Colonel" walked over to Rising Moon and his men and said, "Not all white men are liars just like not all Native Americans are savages."

"We will leave you and your men some blankets, supplies, food and water. The next time we meet I hope we can share each other's company as friends and not enemies. I have left your rifles over there by that tree. When you wake up you will be able to untie each other."

With that, William, Brana, Axle, Lindsey, and Blake stood behind each warrior and Rising Moon yelled what do you mean by "Wake Up"? They were then put into a deep sleep.

They always had the best of intentions but were having to pay for the cruelty of men that had taken advantage of, lied to, and killed the Indians without provocation. The Colonel knew this would be a long hard road to proving themselves before it got better.

They made their way across most of the country without incident. There were small bands of trouble every now and then, however nothing they couldn't handle easily. On their way back east, they were approaching Cumberland Gap, which was a trail blazed by frontiersman, Daniel Boone in 1775. The gap was the best crossing at the intersection of where Kentucky, Virginia and Tennessee came together. They were traveling through a small narrow strip of road when suddenly a shot rang out and then another. Toby Tyler Stevens (wagon driver) fell from his wagon dead. He had been shot straight though the heart. The Colonel could hear the horses of the shooter (s) galloping away! He ordered Thomas and Tasha to give chase but they had already gone. The Colonel picked up Toby and placed him in the back of one of the wagons. What a shame. They were so close. Why, they had not tried to rob them?

Just then, way off in the distance he heard a gunshot and seconds later heard a second one. He could tell by the sound that the shots came from his team and not the killers.

Thomas had no family that the Colonel knew of but he would make inquiries when they got home. He gave the order to make camp for the night. They would bury Toby in a nice spot.

About thirty minutes later Tasha and Thomas came back and reported to the Colonel. Two men on horseback. The first one I killed said his name was Sam Larson. Said he was getting revenge for us killing his brother Tate Larson.

Lindsey spoke up and said, "That's the sodbuster I killed in the saloon." Who was the other man? Don't know came the reply. He drew on me and Tasha shot him. We will get to their horses in a few minutes. We will take them with us said the Colonel. We'll send a dispatch from the next town to the U.S. Marshal what happened. Besides, I don't know exactly which state we are in right now.

In four more days, they reached the Appalachian Mountains and felt a sigh of relief. They were closing in on home.

CHAPTER 16

THE ARRIVAL

In April of 1865, the team of very tired men, women, and horses arrived just west of Petersburg in a small town called Blackstone. They were met by the last of their contacts and given instructions. They would rendezvous in Petersburg at the Centre Hill House where they would receive new orders. There, half their cargo would be loaded aboard the R&P (Richmond and Petersburg) railroad bound for Washington, DC. Washington would be their final stop.

The Richmond and Petersburg Railroad extended for twenty-two miles and linked the two central Virginia cities. The Virginia

General Assembly chartered the company in 1836 and the line was completed two years later. Despite its name, however, the southern terminus of the railroad was in the suburb of Pocahontas, which lay on the north bank of the Appomattox River across from Petersburg. Goods and passengers had to be offloaded and disembarked at the Pocahontas station, and then transported by wagon and carriage across a bridge into Petersburg. Once in the city, the Lynchburg and the Norfolk and Petersburg Railroad linked those two cities.

When the Civil War began (1861-1865), the gap in the rail connection between the terminus of the Richmond and Petersburg Railroad in Pocahontas and the other railroads in Petersburg greatly annoyed Confederate authorities. The gap was deliberate, intended by Petersburg's merchants, to ensure that passengers and freight would have to use local transportation and related services rather than simply slipping through the city en route to other destinations.

As far as the military authorities were concerned, however, the gap was intolerable. In May 1861, the Petersburg Common Council agreed to allow the construction of a rail link provided it was used only for military purposes and was dismantled after the war. On August 14, 1861, the new link opened, and it proved a boon to the rapid movement of troops and supplies between the two cities. The railroad's importance was proved in 1864, the conclusion of the Overland Campaign and the ensuing Siege of Petersburg. In May, Union Major General Benjamin F. Butler launched several attacks against the line as part of his Bermuda Hundred Campaign, but the Confederate forces under General Pierre G. T. Beauregard successfully defended the railroad. Subsequently, thanks to the construction of defensive works around Richmond and Petersburg, the line remained in Confederate control, enabling General Robert E. Lee to shift troops quickly between the two cities to counter Union threats. The Union Commander, Lieutenant General Ulysses S. Grant, constantly tested Lee's and the railroad's endurance by launching attacks. The first was against one city's defensive lines and then the other was between June 1864 and April 1865. Lee successfully parried these thrusts, although he could not prevent Grant from extending the Union lines south and west of Petersburg.

Grant also sought to cut the rail line from North Carolina—the Petersburg Railroad—that formed part of "Lee's Lifeline" and helped supply the Army of Northern Virginia during the ten-month-long Siege of Petersburg. Eventually Grant succeeded, severing the rail communication at Globe Tavern south of the city on August 18, 1864. Lee countered, however, by unloading supplies from trains onto wagons farther south and then transporting them by road to the western end of Petersburg beyond Union-held territory. The tactic worked well until Grant broke Lee's lines and compelled the Confederate evacuation of Petersburg and Richmond on April 2–3, 1865.

At General Lee's insistence, the rail line was extended from Pocahontas across the Appomattox up to the hill near High Street.

Two large concrete trestles had to be built. Lee assured the City of Petersburg there would be no cost to the city. This rail link would be completed in under two months.

The Richmond and Petersburg Railroad had served its military purposes well. Within a short time after the war ended, Petersburg officials took up the tracks that formed the link with other lines.

Eventually, a new railroad line and an improved road system provided continuous transportation between.

CHAPTER 17

APRIL 14, 1865 THE EXPLOSION

Knowing the "Battle of the Crater" had recently taken place in Petersburg with the loss of hundreds of men of both sides, Colonel DeKay expected little if any problems from Rebel or Union troops. Most of the troops were simply tired and just wanted to go home. Petersburg was a beautiful city that offered all kinds of trade and potential growth for families of the period.

The Appomattox river flowed through it allowing for trade of most goods. The Appomattox Iron Works built some of the strongest iron of the day. It was a huge factory located in what is now called Olde Towne Petersburg. The Appomattox Iron Works designed and manufactured many of the parts used to build the CSS Hunley, the country's first submarine used in a war. Once at the Centre Hill House, the Colonel set up camp on the lawn in the back of the house surrounded by beautiful Pecan trees and fields of lush grass. The men were happy to spend a night in the cool Virginia breeze with few mosquitoes. The view from the lawn of the Centre Hill House was enormous and gorgeous from high atop a bluff overlooking the Appomattox river and into the next county. This was a very strategic location because they could see for long distances and spot the enemy long before they approached from land or water. It also offered them several quick escape routes.

But tonight, after a long, nine-month journey, the men were lost amidst song and drink not noticing as the contents of five wagons were emptied into the tunnel.

By morning hearing the usual bellow, they mounted up and assembled. It was then that a few noticed at least half of their cargo had been excised. With a dismissive wave of his hand, the Colonel simply advised this was the first of two drops and that they were nearing the end of their journey. Men and horses, supplies and cargo, were loaded into the empty train cars at the Petersburg station on High Street and were soon under way. Colonel DeKay would stay with the first cargo at Centre Hill, and Captain Povandra would accompany the other cargo to Washington. Crossing the Appomattox River, the train tracks were built on a trestle just over 100-feet above the water.

The trip to Richmond would take about two hours and then they would press on to Washington, DC. The old locomotive was slowly climbing and gathering speed to cross the river. Captain Povandra was a large and friendly man that collected old machines as a hobby and kept them in excellent working order. He also had a large family of nine children. He was walking through each train car checking on the men when a thunderous explosion occurred. The train car lifted high into the air and blew apart into hundreds of thousands of shards of wood, timbers, steel track rails, people and horses. The screams and yells only lasted for a moment until the locomotive and tinder fell into the river, dragging every other car with it. This part of the Appomattox river appeared as one of the deepest as no part of the train could be seen as it sank to the bottom. Only some floating debris could be seen on the water, as other debris had shot into the sky for hundreds of feet and was witnessed by those still standing outside at the Centre Hill House. The explosive fire plume went about 600 feet in the air. None of them had ever witnessed an explosion of this magnitude. Seconds later the heat from the explosion could be felt as far away as Centre Hill.

Windows burst in houses a quarter of a mile away. Downtown buildings shook with a fury. The Petersburg Courthouse vibrated and felt the concussion. Everyone feeling and hearing the blast thought another tunnel had exploded. They then realized the train had just left the terminal. The Train! Everyone ran for the river.

Several bodies and dead horses still floated downstream; all cargo went straight to the bottom. In the days that followed the explosion, divers of the time made many attempts to find the wreckage and cargo but were unsuccessful. They simply did not have the capabilities to dive this deep. Stories were circulated of the "bottomless" river for years. People drowned and their bodies were never seen again. The strong in this area because the land was very narrow here, slimming to about ninety feet wide. This caused the river to continuously dig a trench at the bottom, and over the years, the depth remained unrecorded. Colonel DeKay instantly knew what had happened. Captain Rogers came riding up fast, jumped off his mount, and ran up to the Colonel. He blurted out "Colonel," the whole train just exploded and went in the river. A couple of men were pulled out of the water still alive but badly injured. I am afraid most of them were killed.

"Ok Captain, go back and get me a full detailed report. I want an exact account of who was on the train and a determination of anyone else can be saved," Colonel DeKay ordered.

"Also, was the trestle damaged?"

"Colonel, at first glance it appears about sixty feet of the bridge…, er, I mean trestle went down with the train."

Sounding completely defeated, Colonel DeKay simply said, "Get back to me as soon as you can Captain!"

This tragic loss of friends, trained men, and cargo seemed to take an immediate toll on the passionate man. He simply sat at a table with his face buried in his hands and allowed a small tear to gather in the corner of an eye. He needed to send word to his Commanders.

CHAPTER 18

THE DIG: END OF AN ERA

In the meantime, the Colonel ordered the spare personnel to dig out the tunnel. All day and all night twenty men dug with shovels, pickaxes, and wheel barrels. They were sweating even though the temperature was in the twenties. Fortunately, they retrieved the bodies of three of the soldiers that had passed from suffocation. The diggers only made about six feet of progress. It seemed that with every foot of dirt they moved, at least more two feet fell from the ceiling. Parts of the tunnel continued to collapse as it appeared to be filling in completely. They moved and hauled tons of rocks. Just when they thought they were making progress, the tunnel collapsed, nearly trapping more men. Fortunately, they were able to escape. Colonel DeKay decided to stop digging as he was worried the entire house would fall in on top of the men digging and enough lives had been lost already. In the basement, the door leading to the tunnel was completely crooked and could not be swung wide open. They did manage to get it open about two inches, only to see dirt starting to fall everywhere, completely caving in.

In the morning, a courier arrived with a dispatch from President Lincoln's personal Assistant: Colonel DeKay,

It is with tremendous sadness that I must inform you that President Abraham Lincoln has been shot and killed. The murderer, John Wilkes Booth, is on the run, but armed forces were moving in and should make an arrest very soon.

Colonel DeKay had to let that news sink in for a moment. The sadness was almost overwhelming. His President, and good friend of many years was dead.

The man who wanted nothing but the best for America and all Americans. Lincoln is dead. The explosion of questions in his head was overwhelming. The flood of emotions hit him all at once. He had tremendous respect for Lincoln. He knew the man had loved this country and wanted the best for all. He was the most unselfish man he ever knew. Now, the country would never know just how unfortunate this timing really was. Colonel DeKay was completely devastated. He immediately sent a dispatch to President Davis advising him of the status of the gold and inquiring about new orders. The courier returned two days later with information that the Union Army was searching for President Davis but he had fled Richmond and was in hiding, his whereabouts unknown. The "Colonel" decided to clean up the mess here as much as possible, assemble his team of experts, and find and protect President Davis. Since the war itself was over, The Protectors would take on a new mission that required the use of their skills with Colonel DeKay leading them into many exciting adventures and exploits. The new Director of the U. S. Treasury, William P. Fessenden found a letter in a drawer of his desk that bore the signatures of Abraham Lincoln and Jefferson Davis.

It read:

The bearer of this letter shall know its merit and hold true and confidential that special funding through the United States Treasury has been allocated under the line item budget called "Protectors". This funding shall remain in effect until such time as amended by special Presidential Order.

A separate note attached to this letter explained to the Director that Colonel Arthur B. DeKay (Retired) would be in touch with him very soon and explain the program in detail.

CHAPTER 19

1976 PETERSBURG, VA

Having found the tunnel and finally showing it to the Museum Curator, and subsequently the Petersburg City Manager, Joe explained how (with some embellishment) he came about finding it. The Curator was ecstatic with the find. He immediately recognized the money-making potential for the museum and City of Petersburg.

Six months later, work crews were very delicately digging out the tunnel from under the house and building new wooden supports as they went. They aimed to restore it to look like the original.

During the digging they came upon the skeletons of three men that had died from suffocation of the massive weight of the dirt and rocks that fell on them during the tunnel collapse. Surely, they were killed instantly. But why were they in the tunnel? What were they doing? Beside one of the skeletons was a $20.00 solid gold Double Eagle coin. One of the workers ran to the Curator and showed him the coin.

"What a great find this will make for the museum"! What stories will be told of how it got there."

The state archeological society, Ladies of the Confederacy, and local reporters were all on hand to observe the removal of the skeletons.

They would be reburied with honors in Blandford Cemetery in the Civil War Soldiers section. During the digging, they also found lots of canteens, rifles, ammunition, cannonballs, a cannon and eating utensils. A small wooden crate was uncovered that was   still intact.

They opened it and found mostly old leather shoes and uniforms. The uniforms nearly dissolving when handled. The crate was removed and taken for research.

After several weeks of excavating the tunnel, a worker found what appeared to be another room dug out of a side wall near the basement of the house. As he dug, he soon found himself in a small room, one that had not caved in, but filled with dirt as had the tunnel. There was another skeleton laying on the floor with rotted uniform pants and shirt. Inside the pants pocket gold coins were stuffed inside, and other gold coins lie in a pile on both sides of the skeleton. He died a wealthy soldier. The worker then noticed several entire crates stacked against the walls. Two of the bottom crates had burst open and piles of gold coins had spilled out. Inside, he could see what appeared to be gold bars as well. He started whooping and hollering like a child that just won a ticket to Disneyland. The curator almost fainted with pleasure at the find. This would make worldwide news and he would be famous! Tourists would be lined up to see the tunnel and other artifacts! This would assure the budget needed to build other museums and, wow! His mind was racing one hundred miles per hour thinking of all the possibilities. Little did he know that there were still many more exciting artifacts and gold waiting to be recovered. The burning question he had was "Where did all this gold come from"?

1980 FOUR YEARS LATER

Joe kept reading and rereading his great-grandfather's letter and trying to figure out exactly what the hidden meaning was. One night, during a dream he was having about the letter, he saw the train explode, and fire, men, horses and debris, blowing up high in the air. Then he saw something else. Gold. Lots of gold. Gold coins, and gold bars, flying through the air and splashing down into the river below. He saw the train cars blow apart and trains and track also fall into the river. He could hear the men yelling, but the worse sound was the horses screaming. Cold chills ran down his spine as he felt so badly for them. The river was running very fast in this gorge tonight.

Joe awoke with a start. He knew what he had to do. He looked at his clock and saw that it was 4:00 am. John would be getting up soon so why not call him now? Joe called John and told him to put on the coffee because he is coming over.

"Do you know what time it is? I could sleep for another hour or so."

"When I tell you about an idea that just came to me in a dream, you will be happy to be awake."

At that, John knew to stop questioning. He knew that every time Joe had a dream, he needed to pay attention. Something was about to get real.

John and Joe worked tirelessly obtaining permits, permission, and licensing to use the land on both sides of the Appomattox River. Also, they had to obtain permission from the railroad to use the concrete trestles where the railroad tracks had been years before if needed.

This was the first time in their friendship that Joe revealed to John he had some money saved.

What he wanted to do was going to involve spending a pretty good amount of money, and the worst part would be if they came up empty in their project. They both agreed it was worth a try.

The city had been thankful about Joe finding the tunnel. When the excavation was completed and the tunnel opened to the public, the City had placed a brass plaque at the opening offering thanks to Joe, and the year he found it. That was the end of that. Now, Joe could see if he could make a new discovery. He was pretty sure his great-grandfather was leading him to make more discoveries and, to find the Gold. Joe realized that in the 1800's the technology did not exist to retrieve anything from water of that depth.

They spent weeks preparing the area on both sides of the river. They cut back foliage and made room for bringing up stuff and staging it until it could be inventoried. Arrangements were made for off-duty security with the Petersburg Bureau of Police and The Chesterfield County Sheriffs' Department. The two departments would coordinate security, maintaining men and women on site from the first day of the search until advised otherwise by Joe. An armored car was secured (just in case) as well as the bank to store any valuables that were found. The area had to be cordoned off to keep sightseers back so they would not get hurt. Joe called the U.S. Crane Company and spoke with Greg Shipman. Joe explained he wanted them to deliver two of the largest cranes with Electro-Magnets attached that are capable of potentially lifting a train car full of water and cannon balls from a depth of about three hundred feet. He also wanted their most experienced men to operate them.

When Shipman finished writing up the order, he asked Joe," What in the world are you raising from the bottom, tons of gold"?

They both laughed. "Hopefully some old train boxcars." Shipman asked Joe if he would please send him some pictures and Joe said he would. The cranes would have to be custom outfitted Electro-magnets for that kind of operation, but he would have them ready and delivered in two weeks.

On Friday night, August 15,1980, everything was in place and ready to start. The cranes had been delivered as promised, and they were monsters. The ground had been cleared and it was ready. The entire area was roped off with the proper signage telling people to stay back. The guards wanted fencing, but Joe wanted bystanders to be able to watch as well. All police and guards were in place starting at 6:00 am Saturday morning. Coffee pots would be set up as well as coolers with water and drinks. A temporary power pole was in place as was the all-important Port-a- John. It appeared they were ready.

CHAPTER 21

AUGUST 16, 1980 RAINBOWS END

It was 6:00 am and the river was running very slow today. That was great for us. The temperature was to be in the nineties for a high. Now, it was a pleasant 72 degrees. A few people were already standing along Campbell's Bridge to watch the festivities. The Petersburg Ice House was already in full swing as fishermen were lining up to fill their coolers with ice to go fishing and others to go boating at Lake Chesdin. Some people were simply watching from their cars and trucks to see what was being brought out of the river.John dumped ice in the coolers while Joe spoke with the crane operators. He had filled them in as to what may lay on the bottom and just how deep this channel was. The operators were anxious to get started. This would be a first for both and they were ready to get going. A couple of reporters were there and Joe had set up three video cameras to get three different angles recorded.

Joe, Ernie, and Clarence wore headsets so they could communicate with each other. The men could hear all the conversations anytime anyone spoke.

Finally, Joe said "Let's start digging"!

The cranes' engines were started. Joe pushed a remote button and all three cameras started recording.

"Are you as nervous as I am?" John asked Joe.

"I'm glad we brought the Port-a-Potty because I think I just might shit my pants."

Slowly the cranes lowered the Super XM-440 Electro-Magnets capable of lifting 25,000 pounds each into the water.

The operators called out: "Fifty feet, one hundred feet, one hundred fifty feet, two hundred feet, two hundred fifty feet. Now, both John and Joe's stomachs were in their throats. They were really hoping the water had not gotten too deep for the cables. John looked around. A crowd was already starting to assemble. The local newspaper had ran an article about the excavation and curiosity was everywhere.

At 280 and 285 feet, both magnets landed on top of something and stopped. Ernie yelled out to Joe that he was energizing the magnet, as would Clarence. Ernie had confided in Joe and John earlier that the cables could lift 30,000 pounds each, but they did not want to try it with one crane, with the river current. With magnets energized, they started to lift. The booms on the cranes were bending slightly under the weight. Suddenly, the cables came to a screeching halt.

Both operators stopped the lift.

Ernie yelled, "What do you want to do?"

John answered, "Just let it down, and then pull back up.

Whatever is down there has been in the mud a long time. Maybe we can ease it out or break the suction."

"Just try easily."

Ernie and Clarence started again. Up then down, up then down, nothing.

"Well, pull it tight, and just hold it for a minute," offered Joe, "Let's see if that might break it loose." OK but if we bend these cranes you're going to pay for them. Joe said ok let's go.

Just then, Ernie and Clarence both said, "It's beginning to rise a little!"

Very slowly, the cables began to rise. They were pulling very lightly, just enough to keep pressure on the object. The cranes were straining under the weight. The engine RPM'S were running up. Black smoke was rolling out of the engine exhaust. Suddenly, a something broke the surface of the water.

It appeared to be rusty metal of some sort. Joe and John were looking with great excitement. Just as suddenly as it appeared, it started to sink back under.

Joe radioed Ernie and Clarence, "What's going on?"

Clarence yelled back that it was an unknown force pulling it back down. Both operators released the cable tension so the boom part of the cranes would not bend the frames. They let out about five feet of cable and slowly stopped. The object was bouncing a little in the current. Ernie did not like this strain on his equipment. He told Clarence to let the engines and cable cool down a moment before they started pulling again.

Ernie asked if maybe this thing, if it is a boxcar, has gotten full of sand and rocks over the years. Joe said that would be certainly possible, but he thought the equipment could lift it.

"You're not going to bruise my ego. My equipment can lift it if I can clear the obstructions."

Ernie told Clarence, "Alright now, let's get this thing out of the water and onto dry land. They slowly started to lift the object. Soon, it broke the surface and just kept coming this time.

"My GOD!" John said, "It is a boxcar."

The name of the railroad was gone and it had a lot of rust because it was mostly metal frames and wood sides. It was bent and damaged from being blown up. The sliding door was gone. Water was still gushing out. Thinking out loud, Ernie said, "If it is this heavy in the water, what will it weigh when it comes out?"

"Yeah," Clarence said, "I was thinking the same thing. We better keep the load balanced between us."

Ernie agreed and they moved the boxcar over to the staging area. Everyone around the site was yelling and making noise like it was King Tut's Tomb. It was a truly amazing sight. The cables and frame were creaking loudly; this was a lot of weight with the wooden car soaked with water.

Ernie told Joe there appeared to be something inside.

"I can't see anything," Joe said back to Ernie, "John, do you see anything?"

John was standing closer to the staging area and had a better view.

"Yes, I can see some large object but I cannot tell what it is." The magnet on Ernie's crane suddenly lost all power and the side of the boxcar dropped straight down. Clarence cut power to his, so his crane would not break under the weight. The boxcar dropped and landed upside down in the staging area. A large cannon and lots of cannon balls fell out of the boxcar. The wheels were rotted and broke off when it hit the ground.

"Holy shit!" John said.

"You can say that again," Joe shouted. Of course, John said, "Holy Shit" again. What happened?

Ernie was already out of his cockpit and tracing all the wires. There was a master plug near the end of the boom that had apparently come loose, just enough to break all electrical contact. He put it back together and then secured the wires with short cables that could not be pulled apart by mistake. He and Clarence then did the same to Clarence's machine. They took a break and everyone (including police) walked over to look at what they had. Since the car was upside down and broken, they had to move easy. There was lots of mud and rock inside but there was also artillery cannons, cannon balls, kegs of black powder, Springfield rifles, and several cases of bullets. Most of these were in decent condition because they were covered in mud. These would look great in the museum! The reporters were steadily taking pictures and calling their bosses with the news.

"We will need some help getting this stuff cleaned, " said Joe to John. John said, "Well I guess the State Archeological Society will be along sometime today to try and relieve us of that duty. Joe said well it might just be the best thing.

He replied, "How about I call some friends to bring a truck and take it to clean it. Joe agreed readily. They took a break until John got off the phone, saying help is on the way.

His nephew CW was coming with some friends. Very trustworthy people. Joe really liked CW. He was a good person, liked to have fun, and enjoyed working hard when he needed to.

Joe laid out a grid for the magnets to follow. He did not want to miss something because they did not cover the area properly. They lowered the magnets again. This time they went to almost three hundred feet before they hit bottom. The magnets were energized and brought to the surface. They had a lot of twisted metal, broken hasps off doors and locks, and a couple of rails for the tracks. These were bent really bad, and were rusty. They dropped all the items a little farther out in the staging area away from the boxcar.

John noticed a glint of color in the pile. He walked over and picked it up.

"Damn!" he said, "Joe look at this."

He had found a single $20 gold coin from 1863. I sure hope there are more down there. But if not, I'm happy we found one. Joe told Ernie and Clarence the news and said, "Let's do this again."

They moved a little farther down the grid this time going with the flow of the rivers current. They hit something at 275 feet; it was another very large and heavy object. Ernie did not think it was stuck in the mud this time, just very heavy.

They were able to bring it up about thirty feet when it fell off and the cables, booms and magnets bounced about fifteen feet.

"Good Grief!" exclaimed Clarence. What happened now?

Ernie said the object was too heavy and they didn't have a good enough hold on it for the weight.

"Let's try again."

They lowered the cables and struck the object again. They energized the magnets and started to lift, very slowly, and the object started moving. It was so heavy that it started pulling the boom frames down. Ernie told Clarence to watch his boom and make sure it did not start bending.

"If it bends, we both will cut power to the magnets. Got it Clarence?"

"You bet!" answered Clarence, "I think this load is heavier than the last. Maybe we have a piece of the trestle or something. If we get it to the surface, we will find out soon enough."

In the meantime, CW and several friends arrived with a large wooden stake body truck. They were impressed and knew what needed to be done. They would load these artifacts up then wait to see if there was more on the next load coming up from the bottom.

Just then, Ernie told Joe something was breaking the surface. It appeared to be another upside-down boxcar. The cranes were struggling to pick it up out of the water. Gears were grinding and belts were squealing. Ernie told Clarence to stop a minute.

"We need to let everything cool off. If the boom starts to bend, drop the load.

If it bends, Joe said, "I'll buy you a new one."

Ernie just laughed. He had no idea that Joe was serious. After a few minutes Ernie said, "Alright, let's try this again."

The load was holding strong to the magnets. Ernie's magnet was securely on the bottom of the boxcar frame but Clarence's was on the side of the wood. Ernie figured it must be all metal on the inside to make this magnet hold like that. Ernie told Joe that it was too heavy to lift completely out of the water, but maybe they could drag the boxcar onto the land and then the staging area. Joe told Ernie to do whatever he thought would work. The side doors were still closed on this boxcar, but water was gushing out of it from both sides. Ernie figured that was one reason it was so heavy. The doors were holding the water in under water. They dragged it over to the staging area which worked better than Ernie thought. He dragged the boxcar over and slowly set it down in the staging area and released the magnet unhooking it. At first it appeared the doors were wedged shut even though they were on rollers.

But upon closer inspection, Joe realized they were locked from the inside. Joe looked at CW and asked him if he had anything with him that might be used to pry open the sliding door. CW was already headed toward his truck.

"I've got just the thing."

CW arrived with a huge pry bar with a seriously wide flat blade.

"This should do the trick," he said.

"Yep," John said, "And we don't want to tear it up more than we must. That wide blade should help a lot. CW placed the blade in the opening and three of them started to push. At first it would not budge, then little by little it started to open. When the door neared the opening, gold coins poured out onto the ground. Hundreds of them. All three started yelling and hollering but continued to push on the door. It moved about another eight inches and then stopped. It would not budge now, pry bar or not. John and Joe just looked at each other for a moment. Then John got a huge smile on his face and so did Joe.

"Do you have any idea what these are worth?" Joe said, "I suspect millions."

Ernie and Clarence were also jumping up and down raising and lowering their arms. The Armored Security people came over with buckets and cloth bags to start loading. Joe got his flashlight and climbed into the boxcar with help from CW and his friends. John was supervising the coin collection and he and the two guards were keeping an accurate count.

Joe noticed leather boots, belts and buckles from long dead soldiers. He had to push more coins out so he would not step on them and bend them. He got most of them out of the doorway when he realized what was holding the door. Several gold bars had fallen and were wedged between the door style and the car frame. He picked up a bar and was in awe at how heavy it was. He handed it to John.

"Bring me a bucket," said Joe. He put six bars in the bucket and could hardly lift it. Handing it over to a guard, he told John there were about six hundred more of those gold bars.

"I think we are going to need a bigger truck and more guards."

The guards took care of that request. Joe saw three human skulls laying in a corner eerily staring at him. CW and his men were busy helping the armored car guards count and load the coins and now bars.

Joe looked at Ernie. "That car must have weighed seven to eight tons."

Ernie agreed, saying, "I thought it might be full of cannons and ammunition. It was all my cranes could do to bring it up. Part of the problem was we could not get a firm flat grab with the magnets.

We only had the car by the frame. We got lucky."

For the next several hours the cranes brought up debris, train parts, rail, gold and more. The State Archeological people showed up to say they were going to file a claim for the artifacts to include the gold. Joe was ready for that. His lawyer had prepared all the necessary documents to allow Joe and John to continue to excavate until they decided they were complete. The local Circuit Court Judge had agreed to allow the excavation under the order that everything excavated had to be stored by Joe and John at a secure location until the Fourth Circuit Federal Court could make a ruling on ownership.

They worked for the next three days bringing up artifacts and gold. The crowds of people had swelled in numbers to two hundred. They watched the process from the bridge hollering every time something was brought up. They had filled two armored trucks and was still finding loose coins. They also found a fortune in Henry repeating rifles, Springfield rifles and cannon balls.

Clarence told Joe that he had a screening device that attached to the cables that they could use to scrape the bottom for loose artifacts. John and Joe told him to get one for each crane. The next day when it appeared that most artifacts had been retrieved he attached the scrapers and they went back to work.

Amazingly, they started bringing up piles of gold coins and bars. They also brought up several skulls that Joe immediately turned over to the State. That brought the excavation back to being real. The fact that many men had lost their lives on that train.

There was no way to tell how each family was destroyed by the loss. John looked at Joe and said I think if we end up with some of this money we should make every attempt to find any direct living descendants from those that lost their lives in this wreck. Just another reason we are good friends. We think a lot alike.

EPILOGUE

The "Protectors" continued to work under the direction of Colonel DeKay. Volumes could be written about their exploits using their skills and abilities in protecting Presidents, dignitaries, executives, and yes, even an occasional politician. Even though the

U.S. Treasury Directors changed often, the budget for the Protectors was never in question. It was funded every year. In a secret hallway in an underground level of the U.S. Treasury building, photographs are displayed of all the Protectors including the "Colonel" since its inception in 1862.

"Do they still exist?"

Only the director knows for sure and whoever it is, probably won't talk about it.

1985

SUMMER

PETERSBURG, VIRGINIA

Joe sat in his living room thinking about the events of the past few years. It was 7:00 am and he was missing the excitement of the hunt. How the information just kind of developed over time. It took five years for all the legal battles to be settled. The state said they owned the gold because it was found in a Virginia river. The feds said they owned the gold because it was taken from the mints. The insurance company that insured the gold through the mints said they owned the gold because they had insured it in 1862 for $400 million dollars collectively. And of course, the railroad thought they should own it because it was still on their train (even though at the bottom of the river).

At the Federal Hearing, Joe and John argued that they should be entitled to a portion because it was entirely their investigation that led to the find. The gold had been at the bottom of the river for over one hundred twenty years and nobody attempted to find it. It would still be there had it not been for their efforts. After all, Joe also laid out more than $60,000 in cash retrieving the gold. No one ever offered to reimburse his money. The split of treasure is fairly well defined by the federal courts but not entirely. The Armored Truck Company still possessed the gold bars and coins in their vault until the final court decision, which was on Wednesday, May 15, 1985.

<u>Here is the breakdown:</u>

Net worth of gold bars and coins collectively: $2.2 billion dollars

Lloyds Insurance Co.	**$400,000,000**
State of VA	**$400,000,000**
C & P Railroad	**$100,000,000**
United States Federal Government	**$100,000,000**
J & J Excavations	**$1.2 Billion**

What a payday! Far more money than either John or Joe was expecting. The very first thing they decided to spend was to create a

$200,000,000 college fund for young entrepreneurs with a hired trustee to award scholarships. The two leased a building in the "Old Town" area of Petersburg for their offices and hired a very competent secretary to answer the phones. They added an office administrator and paid her very well to run their business. They had located most of the relatives of each person that died on the train. They made a substantial donation to each family as a whole to divide as they saw fit.

Joe started thinking about his great-grandfathers' letters and went into the home office where he kept the oak box. He pulled out the letters and reread a few of them. Just as he was placing the letters back in the box and putting the box back on the shelf, he dropped the box. He bent down to pick it up and noticed a seam along the bottom of the box that he had never seen before. He touched the seam and a hidden compartment slid open. Inside was a very old piece of folded paper. Carefully, he opened the paper and looked at it for a few minutes. A huge smile came across his face.

He sat back down at his desk and grabbed the wall telephone and dialed John's home phone number. John answered on the third ring.

"Hello," he answered.

"John, pack your bags, we're going to Phoenix, Arizona!"

The End

Coming soon: Finding the Lost Dutchman's Gold

SAMPLE JAMES B. ARNOLD'S NEXT BOOK:

FINDING THE LOST DUTCHMAN'S GOLD

BOOK #2 OF THE

TUNNEL OF GOLD SERIES

The "Colonel was a man of many talents. He is still called "Colonel" even though he retired from the Confederate Army several years ago. The "Colonel" was a man of great integrity and lived by the code of "Do unto other as you would have them do unto you". His dress code was impeccable and his every movement commanded respect. He always thought every man and woman in America should be treated as equals in every way. However, he was in a minority with such thoughts. Men would scoff at him when he made statements such as "Women are just as smart as men" so why can't they vote? They teach all grades in school, but you want to argue about their place in society and at home. He would also say that every man of every color should be provided all the same opportunities as every other man in America. It is ridiculous to think a man of any color is just not as capable as a Caucasian man. But he was a Virginian and he decided to fight where he was most needed and hoped he was fighting for the right reasons: To keep the country united.

His team was known as the "Protectors". Eight men and women, each of whom possessed skills, abilities, and talents that set them apart from most normal individuals.

The "Protectors" took on jobs from the government that could not be handled through the normal course of business.

The "Colonel" always had final word and approval for a mission, no matter what. Only he knew all the capabilities of each member of his elite force and he would never compromise any of them to please a governmental entity.

While on a special presidential expedition during the Civil War, the Colonel and his team met a man near modern day Phoenix, Arizona that appeared to be in great distress. He was at the base of a mountain range known as the Superstition Mountains. He looked as though he had not eaten in days and appeared very dehydrated, as water was scarce. The "Colonel" had him lie down in one of his covered wagons and gave him water. When he could speak, he told the 'Colonel" his name was Jacob Waltz and he was from Germany. Worn and raggedy, Jacob told him he had come to these mountains searching for gold. He was short even by the standards of the average man of the day. At about 5' 3" in height and 95 pounds, soaking wet, he piqued the "Colonel's" interest so much that he told the rest of the team to go ahead to Denver where he would catch up with them. He wanted to stay with Jacob for a couple of days and get him well. The team proceeded on to Denver leaving behind the beef stew they had prepared for supper for the "Colonel" and Jacob. The "Colonels" first name was Arthur and insisted Jacob call him that. Jacob said that for some reason the people of the area called him the "Dutchman" and he did not know why but asked Arthur to please call him Jacob. Jacob had already taken a "shine" to Arthur and wanted to get to know him better as well. He could tell that Arthur was a man of integrity and kindness, traits that he had forgotten existed in this land. He seemed to always be around cutthroats, thieves, and liars. Anytime he went into town the people that saw him, their only interest was wanting to know if he had any gold (so they could rob him) or if he had found any gold. It had been a long time since he met an honest and respectful man. He almost forgot that people like Arthur existed.

What a shame, he thought. Arthur fixed Jacob a large plate of beef stew and gave him a full canteen of water. Jacob was mighty pleased to be eating real food that had been prepared by someone that knew how to cook. Just by the smell he could tell it was going to be good.

The two men sat down on a log and Jacob took his first of many bites and exclaimed, "Oh Mercy! It's been a long time since I put anything that tastes this wonderful in my mouth. Who in tarnation made this stew? Was it that purty girl you called Lindsey? Purty and can cook too."

Arthur looked at Jacob and smiled, "This was my ma's stew," said Arthur.

"She taught me to cook when I was knee-high to bullfrog. I do enjoy a good meal. Now there's plenty so you help yourself Jacob."

Arthur looks over at Jacob and Jacob looked like he had seen a ghost.

"You mean YOU cooked this delicious stew? Why if I was a little more partial to men than women, I would have to marry you myself!"

With that they both busted out laughing. Jacob said he could do with a little more if Arthur really did not mind. Arthur responded by scooping up another big mess of the stew and gave it to Jacob, with a piece of bread to go with it. Jacob simply could not stop smiling.

After a few moments of silence Arthur asked, "Jacob, why are you still smiling?" Jacob said, "Oh, I'm sorry, it's just that of all the people that could have come along and found me, most would have left me and taken my horse, gun, and what money I have. You and your team came, stopped and helped me, and befriended me," Jacob explained.

"Believe me when I say, that is no small measure of luck in these mountains. The scalawags are everywhere."

Arthur asked Jacob, "How did you come to be up here in these hot mountains with no water and no food? You don't strike me as being a person that goes out in the wilderness unprepared."

Jacob said, "A few days ago, I was headed to my claim and I kept hearing someone behind me, so I stopped, got off my horse and pretended to strike it rich to see if they would show themselves. And they did."

Continuing with his tale, Jacob said, "Two nasty varmints from town must-a saw me in the saloon in town and followed me out here. They knew I had some money from prospecting and figured they would kill me and take my gold. Well, they just about killed me, shot a hole in one of my canteens, and then took the other three."

"They scattered my food to the wind and left me for dead," Jacob said shaking his head, "Then, they run off my mule, luckily, I was able to find her the next day. She loves me. She was not going to go too far since the normal watering holes have dried up this year from the heat and no rain at all. They beat me up pretty good, and like I said, they left me for dead."

"Two days later, you come along, Jacob's face brightened. "I got to be the luckiest man on earth."

Arthur responded, "Well, I'm just glad we found you when we did. We never would have if it had not been for the eagle that flew this way. He flew down low over my team three times. I figured that as an omen that he wanted to be followed. He led us directly to you."

"I believe the creatures of our world are a lot smarter that we think, said Arthur, "I also think they know the difference between a good person and a bad one."

Jacob said, "You know, maybe you are right. I have seen animals do some strange things in my time."

With that Arthur went to the wagon and got out an extra bed roll for Jacob and handed it to him.

"Now you can sleep in the back of the wagon if you like."

But Jacob shook his head and said, "I would prefer to sleep right out here under the stars."

They both laid out their bedrolls and put another log on the fire.

Arthur said, "Jacob, I have enjoyed our conversation tonight.

In the morning, I will accompany you to Phoenix and help you get resupplied."

Hearing Arthur say these things brought a tear to Jacob's eye. He started to speak but found he had lost his voice again. He waited a moment and the cleared his throat.

"Arthur, I thank you for your help and hospitality. You are a mighty good man. I wish I had known you all my life."

Jacob then rolled over and went to sleep. Arthur laid there for a few moments thinking about how Jacob's life was so different than his own. Jacob seemed to be a good man, but trouble followed him and tried to get him down.

In the morning, they awoke to the fresh clean scent of the scrub oaks and beef stew. Jacob immediately asked was the stew for breakfast as well? Arthur laughed and said, "Of course, help yourself!"

Jacob retrieved the two plates they had washed the night before and scooped up some stew for them both which just about emptied the stew. As they were packing up Arthur heard a noise in front of the wagon about 150 feet. He told Jacob to stay behind the wagon as he thought he heard people.

"Be careful," Jacob said, "It's probably those scalawags come back for my gold!" Arthur eased out behind the wagon, staying very low. He was trying to get out of sight of the wagon and get into a position where he could see who was out there. Easing around in the scrub bushes, finally, he saw them. Immediately, he figured they must be the men that hurt Jacob, by the way he had described them and their clothes. One of Arthur's unique abilities was that he could tune his ears to pick up sounds from a distance and today, he could hear the men talking about Jacob and his gold mine. They were saying that the gold had to be very close and they were conspiring on how to get it if it were the last thing they did.

Just then, Arthur leapt out, shouting for them to leave while they still could.

"I don't want any trouble...it's time you get on your way home."

One of the men was dressed in all leather buckskin complete with tassels. He turned around, pulled out his gun, and pointed it at Arthur. In the same moment, Arthur pointed his gun and fired. The bullet struck Mr. Buckskin just above the bridge of his nose, and went out the back of his head, taking skull and brains with it. There he fell, right in the same spot where he stood.

The second man had his hand behind his back and yelled, "I only have a knife, don't shoot me!"

Arthur yelled back, "Well, let me see your hand and then walk straight to me."

The man started walking toward Arthur, "Don't come any closer until I see your hand!"

The man said, "I told you I only have a knife!"

Then he turned and drew the gun he had been holding and pointed it at Arthur. In the blink of an eye, Arthur fired his gun and placed the bullet neatly between his eyes as well. Threat eliminated! What a shame Arthur thought, two lives ended in an instant because of greed and because they had evil in their hearts. Arthur walked over to the two men and then called for Jacob to come join him.

Jacob ran down the hill and saw the men and said, "Yep, that's them. I guess they won't be robbing and beating anyone else!

Arthur said to Jacob, "Let's put them on their horses and take them to town with us."

Later, when they were on their way to town Jacob said, "Arthur, that was some mighty fine shooting! I don't think I have ever seen the likes of that before."

Arthur said, "Well, I have been around guns all my life. I even traveled with a friend that sold Colt guns around the country for a while. You do anything long enough, you're going to get good at it."

They rode along in silence for a while. Then, Jacob finally said, "Arthur, I would like to thank you for everything you have done for me."

Arthur said, "It has been my pleasure, Jacob."

As they rode along, Jacob looked at Arthur and said, "I have something to show you. It's something I have never shown another living soul."

He reached in his vest pocket and pulled out a piece of paper and handed it to Arthur.

"Can you read it?"

Arthur stopped the horses and studied the paper.

"It appears to be a map of these here mountains", Arthur said. Jacob was smiling from ear to ear, "That's right!

Then Arthur asked, "What's the map lead to?"

"Gold," answered Jacob, "It's my gold map. It leads to the largest gold mine in history."

Arthur stared at Jacob.

"Well, it's not really a mine, but more of a hole in the ground, and along the walls of the mountain. I swear, it is the richest gold deposit I have ever seen! Some of the nuggets are as big as my fist and are just laying right on the ground! I only take a few small nuggets into town, a few at a time. I have hidden the rest in plain sight, but I've disguised them well."

Jacob said his simple clue to finding the largest nuggets is: Look in plain sight. It is where it should be, but really, it is where it should not be. Hee, hee, hee," he laughed at himself.

"Why?" questioned Arthur, "Why are you showing me your map and telling me your clue? You are the most honest men I have ever met."

"There is more gold in that mountain than I could ever collect even if I spend a lifetime, more gold than WE could spend in a lifetime."

"You saved my life. It's just me. I don't have a wife or children to give this to, so I am telling you this because I would like you to be my partner and share this gold."

Arthur told Jacob, "I appreciate your offer. It is extremely kind, but I cannot take your map. I have another one just like it. Made myself two just in case I lost one."

"Again, that is extremely generous of you. " Arthur said softly, But Jacob, I am not a miner. I am a government worker and I am on a very secret mission right now. Plus, I truly have all the possessions I could ever want."

But Jacob was stubborn, "I want you as my partner and will not take no for an answer. I will do all the mining and will put your half in the bank of Phoenix for you. If you don't want it, well, you can just give it to a charity?

Those guys get greedy, just like the two on those horses behind us. They will spend all the money themselves."

"If something happens to me, you can find the gold using this map. Please keep it safe, Jacob insisted.

"Who knows, I might lose mine and come looking for you to give me your copy."

"It sounds like you have been there many times but you can't remember where it is?"

"The gold is in a location that you could be standing five feet from the entrance and never see it. Part of it lies in a crevasse so tight, I can barely get to it. No one can see it except during certain times of the day when the sun hits it just right."

Arthur spoke as he and Jacob moved on. He shared where he lived in Virginia and invited Jacob to come see him sometime. Jacob promised he would. Soon, he stopped and got off his mule, and ran over to an odd-shaped rock, pushing it out of the way. He picked up a few things and slowly walked over to Arthur holding out hands. Just then, Jacob showed Arthur some of the largest gold nuggets he had ever seen.

Jacob looked at Arthur and said, "I have them hid all over the place. I told you. Look how big they are."

Arthur said, "Well, I guess you need to break these up into smaller nuggets before you get to town."

"No," Jacob responded, "I am going to quit hiding my good fortune. I plan to take these to the Assay Office just like this. Can I give you one of these as a token of our friendship?"

Arthur shook his head, "Thank you Jacob, but I leave the gold to you. Your friendship to me does not come with any price but honesty."

"You are a far better man than people know, he said, "Still, I am putting this one in savings for you," as he held out the largest one.

When they got to town, Arthur stayed with Jacob as far as the

Assay Office and they bid their goodbyes. Arthur deposited the two dead men at the Sheriff's Office.

As soon as the sheriff walked out to inspect the dead, he looked at them and said, "They are both wanted for robbery of a stagecoach. There is a $500 reward offered for bringing these two in. Would you like to wait for the money or where can I send it?"

Arthur thought hard for a moment then looked at the Sheriff, "Does a local church have a donation box where they provide for people during unfortunate times?" The Sheriff assured him that they sure did.

"Well, how about giving it to the church in the name of Jacob Waltz. The Sheriff agreed taking down Jacob's name saying he'd make it happen when the reward money came in. Arthur then walked out to his horse. The Sheriff came out and asked him, "Are you Mr. Waltz?"

"No," Arthur said, "No sir. The name is Arthur DeKay. The Sheriff looked at Arthur and said, "Well, Mr. DeKay, thanks for capturing these two bandits and for the church donation. I don't know many people that would spend their money like that. That's very generous."

"Well, Sheriff, a lot of people are having serious financial problems that I don't have. I hope they use it wisely."

The Sheriff nodded his head and again said, "Thank you, Mr. DeKay, it's been a pleasure making your acquaintance."

Look for this next book, released SOON on Amazon.com

ABOUT THE AUTHOR

James "Jim" Arnold is a Petersburg, VA native. Born there 66 years ago, he grew up near the Petersburg National Battlefield where Civil War soldiers fought for more than a year. As a child, he played among those hills collecting relics of bullets, belt buckles, and uniform buttons from both the North and the South.

As a young man working for the G.M. Clements Painting and Remodeling Company in Petersburg, he discovered the mysterious hidden tunnel that became the cornerstone for his first book in the Tunnel of Gold series.

The native Virginian became a police officer in Petersburg and spent his career moving about the south holding ranking positions of Patrol Sergeant, Detective Sergeant, Deputy Chief and Police Operations Commander. He became Chief of Police for the City of Isle of Palms, SC, and later, Public Safety Director. He also served a short stint as Chief of Police in Spearfish, South Dakota

An avid reader, Jim is drawn to authors Clive Cussler, Lee Child, Michael Creighton, Heather Graham and C.J. Box. He is a motorcycle and Hot Rod enthusiast, and he enjoys scuba diving, sky diving, flying, shooting, snow skiing and writing. An adventurer, he and his wife, Brana, a local attorney, love to travel and have explored the US extensively in the last 20 years, with their adopted six children, ages 10-16. Jim also has two children from a previous marriage, ages 30 and 32, and five grandchildren.

Jim Arnold has been interviewed about his police work, appearing on two magazine covers, and highlighted by USA Today during the 1989 Hurricane Hugo and a child kidnapping case.

CONNECT WITH JAMES B. ARNOLD, JR.

Website
www.JamesBArnold.com

Facebook
www.facebook.com/JamesBArnold

www.TunnelofGold.com

www.ingramcontent.com/pod-product-compliance
Lightning Source LLC
Chambersburg PA
CBHW060354180626
46817CB00008B/3015